P9-DOH-411

Dead by Any Other Name

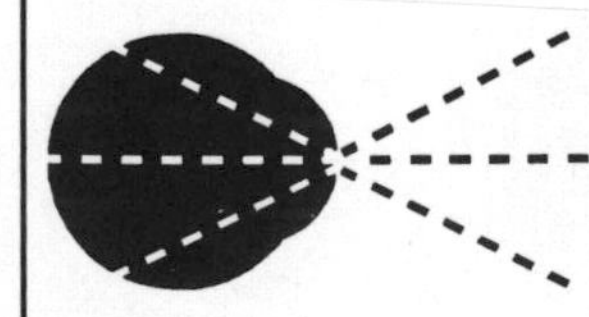

This Large Print Book carries the Seal of Approval of N.A.V.H.

ANET'S PLANET MYSTERY

DEAD BY
)THER NAME

AN STUART

DIKE PRESS
Cengage Learning

either
usly, any
ments,

DATA

n

and

2011037967

imprint of

This is a work of fiction. Names, characters, places, and incident
are the product of the author's imagination or are used fictitio
resemblance to actual persons, living or dead, business establis
events, locales is entirely coincidental.

Thorndike Press® Large Print Mystery
The text of this Large Print edition is unabridged.
Other aspects of the book may vary from the original edition.
Set in 16 pt. Plantin.

LIBRARY OF CONGRESS CATALOGING-IN-PUBLICATION

Stuart, Sebastian.
Dead by any other name : a Janet's Planet mystery / by Sebastia
Stuart.
p. cm. — (Thorndike Press large print mystery)
ISBN-13: 978-1-4104-4340-3 (hardcover)
ISBN-10: 1-4104-4340-X (hardcover)
1. Murder—Investigation—Fiction. 2. Hudson River Valley (N.Y.
N.J.)—Fiction. 3. Large type books. I. Title.
PS3569.T827D43 2012
813'.54—dc23

Published in 2012 by arrangement with Midnight Ink, an
Llewellyn Publications, Woodbury, MN 55125-2989 USA.

For my sisters, Diana Stuart and
Rebecca Stuart,
My cousin, Nicola Montemora,
My sister-in-law, Patti McCauley;
Four fabulous feisty women.

ACKNOWLEDGMENTS

I'm indebted to everyone at terrific Midnight Ink, especially Terri Bischoff, Connie Hill, Lisa Novak, Steven Pomije, and Courtney Colton.

I'd also like to thank Lesli Gordon, Jenny Rose and Dan Boyle, Anthony Rocanello and Chris Tanner, Agosto Machado, Chuck and Patti McCauley, David and Gerry Allan, and Penny Rockwell. And Billy Novotny, who showed what he's made of.

Special thanks to Bob and Babs Malkin, friends, neighbors, and Valleyites extraordinaire.

Gratitude, as always, to the people of the Hudson Valley, who inspire and touch me.

And last, but always first, to Stephen McCauley.

One

I picked up the Elvis commemorative plate — they were common as dirt but this one was kind of cool — a smoldering Elvis leaning against a pink Cadillac in front of the gates to Graceland. I was pretty sure I could sell it to one of my hipster customers, who would display it with pride and irony.

"How much do you want for this?" I asked the woman sitting in the lawn chair sucking down a cigarette and engrossed in a Sudoku booklet.

"Forty," she said without looking up. "It's a collectible."

I put down the plate — which I would have priced at $20 — and moved down the wares table. I spied an orange glass bowl with a sleek oblong shape. This kind of stuff flew out of my shop, especially if I could price it low.

"How much is this bowl?"

"Thirty," Sudoku said, still not looking

up, sucking away. I guess nicotine really does improve concentration. "It's a collectible."

I felt like telling her that used dental floss is a collectible to *somebody.* Instead I muttered "Thanks" and walked back to my car.

It was a gorgeous Saturday morning and I was out yard saleing. Yard saleing ain't what it used to be — the Internet and *Antiques Roadshow* killed it. Now everyone thinks Uncle Gary's "original patina custom bowling ball" is worth eighty bucks and Ashley's circa 2001 pink plastic "limited edition" My First Pony is worth twenty. Well guess what, gang, the market for dead guy's bowling balls is nil, and that "limited edition" numbered a cool million.

Still, I love barreling around to sales — every once in awhile you score a fabulous piece at an amazing price. It's also a great way to observe the flora and fauna in their native habitat. I mean, there's something poignant about seeing Ashley all grown up, dealing with her three kids under five by chugging her morning Bud Lite. And Uncle Gary's heirs unloading his stuff as fast as they can haul it out of his prefab. And then of course there's my so-called business, which needs the inventory. Oh yeah, there was one more cool thing about hitting the circuit — I got to see hidden corners of the Hudson Valley, strange little hollers, tiny riverbank settlements, awesome hilltop vistas.

The back of my van was filled with the morning's haul — a motley collection of fring-frungs and whatnots, half of which I'd probably end up donating to the animal shelter thrift shop. I was just heading over the crest of Cauterskill Road, chugging a cup of coffee, when my cell rang.

"This is Janet."

"Hi, Janet, I'm Natasha. Tosh." The voice was youngish, throaty, inviting.

"What's up, Tosh?"

"I have some jewelry I want to sell. *Masses* of it actually." Then she laughed, a warm laugh that made me like her.

I was getting more into jewelry, mainly because it was so damn easy to deal with — stuffing a sofa into my van was never fun — and if the baubles were at all cool, they sold steadily.

"What kind of jewelry?"

"Well, there's a lot of bakelite, some geometric pieces from my beatnik phase, and a bunch of kitschy animal stuff from when I was in that ridiculous retro phase we chicks go through in high school." The words were pouring out a little too quickly and this time the laugh had an edge of desperation to it. "What *wasn't* I thinking? Anyway I want to unload it pronto, Tonto!"

I immediately smelled a bargain — when people are super eager to sell they rarely want to bother with negotiations, they just want to see some green. This jewelry sounded very promising, I'd take a wad of cash with me and hope for the best.

"So where are you, and what time is convenient?"

"I'm up in Phoenicia and how about now?"

Two

I swung by the shop to drop off my load. I pulled up to the back door, grabbed a cardboard box, walked into my workshop and was greeted by Sputnik's smiling maw and waggling body. Dogs are a direct heart-to-heart charge. With people, it's never that simple.

I dropped the box on my worktable and went out into the store. I pulled the cover off of Bub's birdcage and found the little guy with his head buried in his chest — he liked to sleep late on weekends. He opened his eyes, smiled at me, and then shook himself to full alert. I refreshed his water bottle and he hopped over to it. Lois was asleep on her favorite armchair, the one I was afraid to sell for fear of incurring her wrath. She opened her eyes and glared at me — the Bad Seed in a fur coat.

It was a sunny Saturday in early September, one of the few times customers were pretty much guaranteed in Sawyerville. Luckily the store wasn't my only source of income — I had some savings and since I owned the building and lived upstairs my expenses were low. Still, days like today were important to my bottom line. I sat at my desk, looked around the shop, and felt a familiar stab: *I wish Josie Alvarez were here.*

Josie was the smart, feisty fifteen-year-old I'd hired last spring to help out in the store. She came from an abusive family and had a visible scar to match her emotional ones: one leg was a little shorter than the other because her mother hadn't taken her to the hospital after Josie broke it playing. One day I saw her boozy stepdad slap her and — after practicing my kickboxing technique on his body — I moved Josie in with me until she got hooked up with a foster family up in Troy. She'd only lived with me for a month, but she'd definitely left a mark, damnit. I missed her. And on a practical level, she was just so damn bright and competent and ran the store better than I did. But she was in Troy with her foster family, which was the best outcome for everyone, right?

I picked up the phone and called George, my pal who lived down the street. George was around my age — early forties — an

ER nurse who'd bought up a few buildings in town and was now semi-retired, living off the rents he collected. When I first moved to Sawyerville, he helped me get my shop up and running — he had a great gay eye, was loyal and fun if a bit, well, self-dramatizing at times.

"Listen, I got a call to go look at some jewelry. Can you open the store for me?"

"Damn, babe, not a good morning. I've got company." He lowered his voice. "He's still asleep. And no, I am *not* in love with him. I have learned my lesson. No more absurd obsessions."

"Whatever."

"He trains horses," George swooned. Sawyerville was home to a large horse show that met a half-dozen times a year. "Have you ever heard of anything more romantic in your life?"

I'd only known George for a year and a half but I'd already invested way too much time in his amorous adventures. The man had a neurotic need to be "in love," to focus all his attention and affection on another man. It all sounds very giving and selfless, but after having watched the pattern play out a few times, I'd decided that it was actually a strange kind of narcissism — it seemed like it was all about the love object, but it was actually all about *George.* How passionate, adoring, and giving *he* was.

"When I think of horses," I said, "I think of dust, manure, and *The Godfather.*"

"Janet, do you kill dreams consciously or is it some kind of weird compulsion?" I heard him crunch on his toast. "But *okay,* I'll open for you. I know Antonio — he's Brazilian, doesn't that make you just *melt* — has a morning workout. As soon as I get him fed and on his way, and drop in at Chow, I'll hustle over."

Chow — run by our friend Abba — was the homey restaurant that was Sawyerville's unofficial town hall, nerve center, and gossip mill.

"You're a doll."

"Well, if last night is any measure, Antonio agrees with you in a *big* way."

THREE

I headed west on 212. One of the coolest things about the Hudson Valley is how it's flanked on the west by Catskill State Park: 700,000 acres of green mountains crisscrossed by rushing streams, set up by some smart folks back in 1895. Talk about foresight. The park pumps money into the area; in fact it pretty much *is* the local economy — tourists, skiers, second-homies; I'm told the Catskills are a hiker's paradise (there are no hikes in my paradise). Anyway, I loved driving up into the mountains, all that open country cleared my head, made my chest open wide, my breathing come easier (as long as I didn't have to get out and walk around in it).

I passed through Woodstock, jammed with its usual nut jobs, ancient beatniks, tie-dye survivors, and Saturday morning flea-market crowds. Phoenicia was about twelve miles up past Woodstock, and with each mile you got deeper into the country. I passed a Zen monastery, some fancy country restaurants, and a mix of old farms, modest houses, and richie-rich second homes.

Phoenicia is a loose scruffy little town that sits in a bowl surrounded by mountains. There are streams at every other street corner, nothing is tarted up, the houses tend toward ramshackle, the place feels almost like a Western town in its lack of affect and cutesy gift shops.

Natasha's house was at the very end of a dead-end street. It was a small cabin fronted by a screen porch, barely visible through a thicket of pine trees, vines, and shrubs. No gardener she. I walked down the overgrown path and knocked on the porch door.

"Janet!" Nastasha cried, charging out of the cabin. I pegged her at a skosh short of thirty, with long, lustrous, jealous-rage-inducing black hair, the whitest skin, a quirky, sensual, not-quite-beautiful face that still had a tiny hint of baby fat (I guess by now it was adult fat), all lit up by enormous soulful dark eyes. She was wearing a flouncy skirt, a thick black leather belt, black ballet flats, and a red silk blouse that made her look sophisticated and did nothing to hide her dynamite figure. This gal was stunning, but in a tossed-off, I-don't-really-give-a-shit way that I found appealing. She was also so high-strung and quivery that she seemed to be vibrating. I immediately suspected chemicals were involved.

"Thank you for coming up so quickly," she said, leading me into the house. "I've made us a little berry cake, I tromped around and harvested them myself, and some divine green tea from Cape Verde." She grew still for just a moment and a dreamy look came into her eyes, "I would *love* to visit Cape Verde." In addition to anxiety, she radiated warmth, vulnerability, and a desperate need to be loved. I was charmed. And wary. I sensed Natasha was in trouble, wanted company, someone to talk to. "Unless you're in a mad hurry, that is?"

"I've got a few minutes." I didn't want to blow the deal by being too abrupt, but Natasha was just the kind of complex, screwed-up but *muy sympatico* person who could suck up a lot of my psychic energy — and that was my old life as a psychotherapist, the one in which I was being *paid* to care. I couldn't afford to be this chick's shoulder, for more reasons than one.

The cabin was decorated in off-hand boho chic — a mix of comfy old pieces and mid-century — with a lot of books and CDs; there was a patina of dust and the place was none too neat, several large packing boxes stood in one corner. We sat around the coffee table. She poured me a cup of tea and cut me a piece of cake. Edith Piaf was playing on her iPod.

"So how did you find my number?" I asked.

"I just googled local antique shops and I loved the name Janet's Planet. Sophisticated research, huh? Hey, I love your earrings."

I was wearing my favorite pair — Mexican silver and black onyx. "Thanks."

"I love jewelry, but I need to sell because I'm moving to LA. My little country experiment hasn't worked out quite the way I'd hoped." She ran her fingers through that amazing hair and laughed, but I was sure I saw fear in her eyes. "You know, get out of the big bad city for a while, away from big bad men, big bad drugs, the whole *scene*. Settle down, sober up, get back to writing songs."

"So you're a songwriter?" I asked, unable to control my goddamn trouble-making curiosity.

"Slash-singer. Was. Am. Will be." She picked up a CD from the table and handed it to me. There was a shot of Natasha on the front, looking ravishing and soulful in the middle of a nighttime urban swirl. "I had three CDs before I was twenty-five. I'd like to have a fourth before I'm thirty. I was kind of a semi-name. But a taste of honey triggered a whole lot of crap for me." She laughed in a way that wasn't funny.

What is it about my face that makes people pour out their life stories the minute they see me? Whatever it is, I wonder if there's a plastic surgeon who could erase it. But hey, look, this wasn't costing me anything. I could get up and leave whenever I felt like it. It wasn't like I was hanging on every word, every admission, every emotion. I was here because I needed inventory. End of story.

"So I bought this little place three years ago, but then I got up here and my money ran out. Well, guess what, Janet? Even in the middle of big fat nature, a girl can get herself into big fat trouble. But I'm getting clean and dry and I'm staying on the beam if it kills me. How's the cake?"

I was wondering if the clean-and-dry included prescription drugs — then I realized my wondering was getting a little too acute for comfort, was edging into oh-Christ-I-care-about-this-person. "Delicious. About the jewelry . . ." Hurt flashed across her face. "Hey, I'd love to hear a little," I said, indicating the CD.

"Would you? Would you really?" She got up and fiddled with her iPod. "This is one of my songs — *Love by Any Other Name.*"

The melody was bluesy, soulful, the lyrics both rueful and romantic, and her voice was a dream — distinctive and warm, sexy, with a kick-ass lower register.

"This is great," I said.

She was moving around the room now, swaying to the music, singing along.

I'm no talent scout, but the kid had *it.* Lots of it.

"Oh God, I can't wait to get onstage again," she said. "I'm staying with my friend Vondra in Silverlake for the first few months. I still have some contacts in the business. I'm off my high horse forever, I'll do voiceovers, commercials, back-up, you name it. And I do adore LA, that slightly seedy glamour, the nooks and canyons, the exuberant architecture."

She twirled and hit a note. The song ended and she stood there dazed for a moment. Then she looked down and a storm swept over her face, trouble and fear.

"Are you all right?"

"Me? Oh yeah, sure, fine. And I'll be even better when I've put three thousand miles between me and the East Coast — for more reasons than one," she said, a bitter edge creeping into her voice. I had an urge to ask for more, but bit my tongue. I was *not* a shrink anymore. That was my past. Over. Done. Natasha was in trouble, but it was *her* trouble, not mine.

"I should probably get back to my store," I said.

She disappeared into the bedroom and returned with a wooden box. She put it on the coffee table and opened it, revealing a treasure chest filled with jewelry that I could immediately tell was the good stuff.

"Here it is, Janet, take your pick."

I pored through some pretty serious bakelite pieces — hanging cherries, the iconic mahjong bracelet, geometric pins, rings, earrings. This stuff sold easy-peasy. Then there was a Noah's Ark of animal pieces — charming, kitschy, and they sold, too (chicks *still* go through that retro phase). Finally there were the dramatic silver pieces, all swoopy and mid-century, some with large inlaid stones — this stuff flew out of the store and was tough to find.

"This is great stuff," I said.

"I love it all. It's gonna be hard to let it go. But I need to. Fast."

"So you're not interested in consignment?"

"I need cash."

I wanted to give her a fair price but wasn't sure I could afford to. I'd brought along two grand in crispies, but this stuff was worth at least double that wholesale.

"Well, how does five grand sound for the lot?"

"It sounds fair."

"I can give you two now and the rest on Monday. I'll pick up the stuff then."

"No, take it now. I trust you. And here, have one of my CDs."

As Natasha walked me out to my car, she scanned the street.

"I hope things work out in LA," I said.

"There's a man I'm leaving behind. We love each other, but he's trouble. And so am I. Which adds up to a bad moon rising. Someday he'll understand."

She looked at me and for a second I thought she was going to burst into tears. Then she hugged me. Too tight.

I got in my van and as I drove away I looked in the rearview — Natasha was waving goodbye.

FOUR

When I got back to Sawyerville, I decided to drop into Chow for a quick bite before I took over from George. The joint was crowded with its usual menagerie of retirees, loafers, lowlifes, and hipsters, swelled by Saturday shoppers. I sat at the counter and waited for Pearl to show up. Abba *really* needed to hire another waitress. I mean, shuffling shell-shocked old Pearl with her gray hair, gray eyes, gray teeth, and gray skin gave the place a certain surreal quality — she reminded me of a character in one of those incomprehensible theater pieces they do in the East Village; you know, all striking tableaus and eerie nonsequiturs that add up to something profound and headachy — but as a waitress she was a bust.

Abba saw me through the pass-through and waved me into the kitchen. I joined her. She was putting together about four orders at once, but one of her many talents was the ability to talk and work at the same time. Abba was a few years older than me, a Hudson Valley native — from one of the early black families who settled here in the mid-nineteenth century — and a free spirit who had traveled all over the world. About five years ago she had found herself pulled back, deciding that the valley was where she wanted to be, home again. She was a self-taught chef with a real gift for making magic in the kitchen, drawing on the spices and skills she had picked up in her wanderings. She was also one helluva friend.

"You need to hire some help," I said.

"Hey, Pearl is my good-luck charm, she came with the place and she's staying. But I am looking for a little back-up. How are you?"

"Good, could I get a Cuban sandwich?"

"Coming right up."

"I scored some amazing jewelry this morning." I told her a little about Natasha and then showed her the CD.

"Oh yeah, Natasha Wolfson, George and I saw her perform down in New Paltz about three years ago, she was fabulous. I mean *really* good. There were articles in the paper about her moving up here, she was a rising star. I wondered what happened to her."

"Whatever it is, I don't think it's good.

She seemed really desperate, scared, and probably high, I got the feeling her life was off the rails. She's selling everything so she can move to LA."

"You know her parents are those famous shrinks you always see on TV, what are their names, Howard-and-somebody Wolfson?"

"Howard and Sally Wolfson are her parents?" That was a surprise. The Wolfsons were the authors of a bunch of pop-psychology books, offering up just the kind of shallow, facile, tie-up-all-your-traumas-in-a-nice-silk-bow bullshit that made my blood boil. If I'd learned one thing in my years as a practicing shrink, it's that you *can't* leave your deep hurts behind, you have to work to understand them, make some kind of peace, and then move forward *with* them — but with you, not them, in the driver's seat. The Wolfsons' pabulum led to more unhappiness because it made people feel inadequate, unable to live up to the freedom and happiness that they were claiming was possible.

Pissed me off. I can't tell you how many of my clients would say to me, "I just can't get over my husband leaving me" or "my Mom's death" or "the size of my thighs." My answer was always, "Stop trying." Then we'd get to work understanding their traumas and neuroses, getting a perspective on them (time was an invaluable ally) and then moving forward as alpha dog over the pain and ghosts and nasty little inner voices. People like Howard and Sally Wolfson made the job harder, and if you ask me they're a symptom of a spoiled, narcissistic society that worships at the altar of instant gratification, entitlement, and pat answers.

Finding out they were Natasha's parents increased my sympathy for her by a factor of ten. "Do you know anything else about her or them?" I asked Abba.

"The Wolfsons live down in the Hudson Highlands, in some amazing glass house cantilevered out over the river; it was featured in the *Times* a few years ago. You want to eat this sandwich here?"

"I should take it over to the store. George opened up for me."

Abba wrapped the sandwich and handed it to me. "I'm sure you've heard about his horse trainer."

"Giddyup."

FIVE

There was a commotion out on the street. A lanky man of around forty was making his way down the sidewalk, surrounded by a small entourage, shaking hands, smiling. One of his posse was carrying a sign: Building a *New* New York — Reelect State Senator Clark Van Wyck.

I'd read about Van Wyck in the local papers but had never seen him in person. He was a good-looking guy, athletic, toothy, with a wholesome Vermonty vibe, but — even as he was reaching for hands, waving, shouting a greeting, grinning — he seemed distracted. He was going through the motions but this guy's head was somewhere else.

He reached me and gave me a disarmingly modest smile, "Clark Van Wyck, I'd appreciate your vote."

I shook his hand.

Helen Bearse, a realtor in town, was one

of his entourage. "Janet runs an antique shop just across the street."

"Well, I'm working for *you,*" Van Wyck said, "Folks like you are the backbone of this valley — and this state."

He kept moving. Helen grabbed my hand, "Janet, if Clark wins there's a *very* good chance he'll be elected majority leader. It would be *incredible* for the whole valley. He was born and raised here. And he doesn't want to stop there — his real goal is governor."

I had kind of mixed feeling about the news. Powerful politicians always seem to end up in bed with the greedbags and fat cats, who tend to skew toward real estate developers. I liked the Hudson Valley the way it was and you could almost smell the development pressure. It was hardly an unspoiled paradise, thank God — I loved the crazy-quilt mix of country/suburb/city but I'd sure hate to see it become unbroken sprawl. It wasn't like I wanted to put a fence around the place. Just a gate maybe. If this Van Wyck guy made it to the governor's office, chances are he'd arrive with a lot of IOUs from condo cowboys salivating to leave their mark up and down the valley.

Van Wyck's cell rang and for just a split second a look of panic swept across his face.

He checked the incoming number. “It’s just my wife,” he said, half to himself. “I’ll call her back later.”

Just his wife — hmmmm.

Then he saw another voter and slapped on a smile.

Six

George was sitting at my desk engrossed in *Horse & Rider.* He didn't even look up when I walked in. What if I'd been a customer? I coughed. He shot me a glance and went right back to the magazine.

"Did you sell anything?"

"Horses are *the* most fascinating creatures on the planet," he said.

"At least for the next two weeks."

"Were you born that cynical or is it something you acquired during the nightmare called your life?"

"I can't wait to meet him."

"Oh, Janet, he's a dream walking. Of the earth — earthy. There's something so primitive, primordial, almost prehistoric about the work he does, you should see him with his horses, the bond, it's mythic. He's going to teach me to ride . . . as soon as I get over my terror of horses."

The Sawyerville horse shows ran over long

weekends and the town flooded with horse owners, trainers, breeders, and grooms — when it came to the town's economy it was like someone suddenly turned on a spigot. As for the shows themselves, I'd never been, but it was on my to-do list, right after "read *War and Peace.*"

"I just met Senator Van Wyck out on the street. Sounds like he's going to be the next majority leader up in Albany."

"When you're in love those kinds of prosaic developments don't really matter."

"What do you think of him?"

George closed the magazine. "Actually, I think he's pretty good. He's a green maniac and I think he really cares about the valley. He's rich, or his wife is, so he doesn't need to kiss quite as much ass. I've been doing a little volunteering for him."

George was almost as passionate about his politics as he was about his men.

"Hey, my morning run was pretty productive. Check out this jewelry."

I put the box on the desk and opened it. George's eyes grew wide. "Holy shit, Janet — *score!*"

"Some cool stuff, huh?"

"Wicked cool."

"I bought it from Natasha Wolfson, Abba

said you guys heard her sing a few years ago."

"Oh yeah, she was *amazing.* So soulful. And captivating. She was really vulnerable, a little bit sad and lost. But she poured it all into her music."

I filled him in on my visit with her.

"My friend Tony lives up in Phoenicia and he told me that lately she has the world's hottest boyfriend, just like a total knockout. He sees them around town. He says she seems in kinda rough shape, though."

"Like how?"

"Like high. Either too up or too down. And sort of scared."

"Do you know anything about the boyfriend?"

"Tony's pretty sure he doesn't live in Phoenicia, somewhere down-county maybe." He picked through the jewelry box. "Oh, and look at these fabulous silver earrings! I'm going right down to the jewelers and have them turned into cufflinks for Antonio. He'll adore them, they're so . . . stallionesque! Oh God, I'm starting to smolder."

George leapt up and headed for the door.

"Wait a minute, you still didn't tell me if I had any customers this morning?"

George gave me a pitying look. "Your

crass commercialism offends my soul."

And then he was gone.

Seven

I did have customers the rest of the day and, as I suspected, Natasha's jewelry was popular and I sold half a dozen pieces. That night the valley was rocked by violent storms, at one point a thunderbolt crashed over the town and woke me up — Sputnik jumped up on the bed and curled at my feet. The thunder in Sawyerville always amazed me — it hurtled down the cloves between the mountains and exploded into the valley; according to legend, it was Rip Van Winkle bowling — well, he was rolling strikes Saturday night.

Sunday was another busy day and I slept even later than usual on Monday. Since the store was closed, I lingered upstairs, enjoying my coffee and some quality time with my brood (quality time with Lois meant feeding her). At the civilized hour of 11 AM I called Natasha to arrange to pay her the three grand I still owed her.

There was no answer. I left a message.

A few minutes later the doorbell rang down in the store. I went downstairs — followed by Sputnik with Bub riding rump — and saw Abba outside. She looked disturbed.

"Something very sad happened," she said.

"What?"

She handed me a copy of the day's *Freeman.*

LOCAL WOMAN DIES IN PLATTE CLOVE

The body of Natasha Wolfson, 29, of Phoenicia, was discovered by a hiker on Sunday in the Devil's Kitchen section of the upper Platte Clove. The New York State Police report no sign of foul play and have made a preliminary ruling that the death was either an accident or a suicide; an autopsy has been scheduled. Ms. Wolfson, a singer and songwriter, is the daughter of nationally known psychologists and authors Howard and Sally Wolfson.

Devil's Kitchen is considered one of the most dangerous climbing spots in the entire state. Within the last year alone, two other hikers have fallen to their deaths. According to police, Ms. Wolfson was not wearing hiking boots.

I went a little numb with shock, and then a wave of sadness swept over me. Natasha was a good kid, she was struggling with some serious demons but she had talent, heart, and most of her life in front of her. Not anymore.

"You okay?" Abba asked.

"Yeah."

"She kind of got to you, didn't she?"

"If I let every troubled, mixed-up soul who I spent a little face time with get to me, there wouldn't be any *me* left *to* get."

Abba just stood there for a moment and then said, "Are you or aren't you going to invite me in for a cup of your so-called coffee?"

I nodded.

While I made a fresh pot of my out-of-a-can coffee she scratched Bub's head, sending him into paroxysms of avian ecstasy. Lois kept her distance — Abba had told Lois on more than one occasion that she had no truck with her "haughty bullshit." Cats *are* weird, I mean where do they get the nerve?

I handed Abba her cupajoe, she cocked her head and looked at me with those big amber-green eyes of hers.

". . . Yeah, all right, she fucking got to me," I said. "I mean she was so full of life, she had moxie . . . she sang a little for me, a song she wrote . . . listen to this." I slipped Natasha's CD into my player. Her soulful throaty voice filled the store:

Love by any other name
Would hurt the same

We sat there listening and when the song ended, Abba put down her coffee and gave me a hug. Now hugs tend to bug me, they're the goddamn panacea for everything — "Oh, you chipped a nail, let me give you a *great big hug!*" "Oh, an escaped mental patient slaughtered and ate your whole family, let me give you a *great big hug!*" But this one felt good. Mostly because it was coming from Abba.

"I know you hate these, but tough shit," she said.

I didn't hug back — I mean there are limits.

Thank God Abba didn't do that end-of-hug squeeze thing, that really sends me up a tree. She picked up her cup and sat in a turquoise vinyl armchair that George had pronounced "kitsch chic."

I sat behind my desk. "I'm not sure I buy that it was suicide. I know what that level of despair looks like and Natasha Wolfson was nowhere near it. In fact she was focused on the future in a way that is the clinical opposite of suicidal. And I don't think it was an accident. I was with her that morning, she was way too preoccupied to drive all the way up to the top of Platte Clove and set off on a hike. Plus that kid was less of a hiker type than I am. It just doesn't compute."

"Don't you think the police are looking into every possible scenario?" Abba asked.

"I don't know, Abba, you remember what happened with the Daphne Livingston case."

"I do."

I stood up. "Listen, I'm going to head out."

"Where are you going?"

"Suddenly I'm in the mood for a little hike."

EIGHT

Hiking is one of those activities that sound fun in theory. In reality hikes are a huge fat bore; I know because Zack, my alleged boyfriend, has dragged me on a few. The problem is you're stuck on a trail that climbs through woods, and after ten minutes of tromping it's "oh wow, how exciting, more goddamn trees" (I'm sorry but trees are overrated, they're just ginormous weeds). Then there's the fear factor, especially round about late afternoon when you're stuck on some dark narrow track and you know if you dawdle too long the trees will close over you and the woods will swallow you up and you'll never be heard from again. I mean, do you think it's an accident that in fairy tales the woods are always a metaphor for terror and death? Those Grimm Brothers knew what they were talking about. I'll take a nice long walk around a lake, a swamp, or a strip mine over a hike in the woods.

At least with the Platte Clove — which is a narrow gorge between Kaaterskill High Peak and Plattekill Mountain — there's a rushing stream to distract you. Zack lives in West Sawyerville near the bottom of the clove, and we've hiked up it a little ways in the summer to cool off in one of the swimming holes. But Natasha died at the top, so I drove up the narrow seasonal road that runs above the stream. At the top I parked and followed a trail leading into the woods, toward the heart of the gorge and the stream.

The trail zigzagged downward and then began to run along a wide ledge, I could hear the stream but not see it. A little ways farther the ledge narrowed and then the trail was cordoned off by police tape. I slipped under the tape and walked closer to the lip of the ledge. It overlooked a waterfall that I pegged at about 100 feet high. At the base of the waterfall was a pool surrounded by huge rocks; if you fell you'd smash open your skull like a melon. My stomach turned over. I have this thing about heights — they scare the shit out of me.

I couldn't imagine Natasha throwing herself off this ledge. I suppose I could imagine her slipping, but that would mean she was up here hiking, which didn't seem at all likely to me. I *could* imagine someone pushing her. In many ways, it would be the perfect crime. One quick shove and it's *arrivederci,* baby. No evidence, no clues except maybe shoeprints, and the storm that night no doubt washed those away. I grabbed onto a tree and craned my neck forward for a better view — *whoa.*

"Janet, what the hell are you doing up here?"

I turned around and saw Detective Chevrona Williams of the New York State Police squinting at me, hands on her hips. As usual, she radiated this sexy, understated authority that reminded me of a young Clint Eastwood — if Clint was a black chick. Also as usual, a frisson of *je ne sais quoi* (oh all right, I *sais quoi*) shot through me. Which was weird, since I'm straight (my only lesbo experience was that night in 8th grade when me and Laurie Goldberg stole a fifth of Bacardi from her parents' liquor cabinet, drank half of it, and diddled each other — just when it was getting fun, Laurie puked). At least I think I'm straight.

"Just admiring the view."

"And breaking the law."

I ran my fingers through my curly hair and gave it a quick shake. "Now, detective, has anyone *ever* been prosecuted for crossing police tape?"

"I'm not in the mood for cute."

Well, I tried.

I ducked under the tape.

"Hi," I said.

She remained silent. I thought I detected a little quarter-smile, but clearly she was in no mood for chit-chat.

"I'm not sure Natasha Wolfson's death was an accident or a suicide. I think she may have been murdered," I said.

Chevrona narrowed her eyes and stayed closed-lipped. It always got to me when she did that.

"I spent an hour with her on Saturday. In my opinion she wasn't someone on the verge of suicide."

"I deal in facts."

"A person's psychological state *is* a fact."

"It could have been an accident. This area is called Devil's Kitchen for a reason. See these pine needles? When they get wet they're as slippery as ice. When someone falls on them, they start to slide downhill toward the lip of the ledge and they can't stop themselves. That's how most of the deaths up here happen."

"That would be a terrifying final few seconds, wouldn't it?"

"Yeah, and during the fall itself they may bounce off the rock walls. No pretty corpses up here."

"Even though she lived in Phoenicia, Natasha was a real urban type, I just can't see her hiking up here alone."

She nodded and a little warmth sparked in her eyes. God, she was great looking, with that smooth mocha skin and sleek jawline. Why the hell did I wear hiking boots to go hiking when I could have worn those nice flattering high-heel sandals?

"Have you found any evidence that she wasn't here alone, I mean any fingerprints or shoeprints or anything?" I asked.

"At this point any shoeprints we find will belong to one Janet Petrocelli."

"Oh God, I'm sorry . . . I didn't even think of that."

"This is a crime scene, not a scavenger hunt."

There was something exciting about being reprimanded by Chevrona, she was just so . . . *manly,* in a womanly way. If that makes any sense.

"We dusted for anything we could find, but that storm washed away everything — we came up zippo."

We stood there on the mountaintop ledge for a moment.

"So . . . how's everything?" I asked.

She looked down, rubbed the back of her neck; when she looked up her natural authority was tinged with that sweet vulnerability that made me want to hold her and tell her everything would be okay.

"Things aren't bad."

"Are you —"

"Back together with Lucy?"

I nodded. Lucy was her former partner, who left her for a man.

"No."

There was another pause, filled with her loneliness.

"Okay, listen, do you mind if I poke around a little, up in Phoenicia? Natasha kinda got to me."

"Lotta stuff gets to you."

"Yeah."

We looked at each other — it was *a moment.* Then she looked down and cleared her throat.

"Okay sure, poke all you want. And if you find anything, let me know right away."

"Yes, Sir, I mean M'am, I mean Chevrona, I mean Detective Williams."

She laughed, and it felt like a mountain stream, rocks and all.

NINE

I headed up to Phoenicia, parked in town and, trying to look inconspicuous, strolled up Natasha's street toward her little house. I'd called George's friend Tony to see if he knew anything more about the identity of the man he'd seen Natasha with; the only information he gave me was that "on a scale of one-to-ten, he's a twenty." I was looking for something a little more concrete.

There was her small sad cabin, hidden in its jungle of evergreens and scrubs. I looked up and down the street before I walked up the path to the screened porch. I tried the door, it was open, I stepped inside. The porch had a wicker loveseat and a couple of vintage metal lawn chairs, felt like a place where Natasha hung out — there was a coffee table with a few mugs on it, a Larry McMurtry novel, an iPod dock, candles, incense. No sign of a struggle. I tried the front door of the house, locked. There was a window that opened into the living room, it was open a crack. I pushed it up and clambered inside. Was I breaking and entering? Nah, I didn't break anything.

The living room was bone quiet and looked just like it had two days, just forty-eight hours ago, when Natasha had filled it with her longing, her voice, her fear. Midday light filtered through the surrounding greenery poured into the room, emerald and eerie, the berry cake she had made for us was still sitting on the table. There was a small ashtray with a roach in it; I didn't remember that from Saturday. Maybe the gorgeous boyfriend was a pothead. No signs of a struggle. Just a palpable sense of emptiness, the room felt so much like Natasha — quirky, creative, soulful . . . and gone.

I walked into the bedroom. It was painted a warm rosy beige and was dominated by an enormous bed with an old wool blanket on it. Clothes and shoes spilled out of the closet, the dresser top was covered with jewelry, make-up, fring-frungs. The room was cozy, sexy, girly, haphazard. I opened the dresser drawers and rummaged through the clothes. I looked in the bedside table — just the usual random clutter. I walked over to the shallow closet. She had an amazing array of clothes, ranging from campy retro to exquisite vintage to tossed-off hip. I pushed the clothes aside. There, hanging on hooks on the back wall, was a black leather corset, long black leather gloves, three whips, on the floor in front of them were thigh-high black leather boots with stiletto heels.

It all looked well-used.

Ten

"Toshy, tooshy, whooshy!" the woman's voice cried as the screen door slammed. I pushed the clothes back to cover the S&M paraphernalia and tried to look nonchalant. "Where are you, honeybabe?" The owner of the voice appeared in the bedroom doorway, stopped short — "Oh, hey. Who're you?"

I pegged her for pushing sixty, wearing a long skirt with a zigzag hem, cowboy boots, a billowy blouse, leather belt with a big silver buckle, her hair was bottle blonde, her face lively but raggety and worn, with some serious black eyeliner and magenta lipstick — all-in-all she looked like Stevie Nicks if Stevie Nicks had been waiting tables, smoking Marlboros, and drinking cheap white wine for forty years.

"I'm Janet, a friend a Natasha's."

Her eyes narrowed. "She never mentioned a girlfriend named Janet."

"Um, we're recent friends. I have a store

down in Sawyerville, I'm selling some of her jewelry."

A smile spread across the woman's face and suddenly she radiated a hardbitten warmth, "Oh, shit yeah, *of course.* I'm the one's been telling her to sell that stuff, she needs to cash outta here, baby. Course I'm gonna miss the motherfuck out of her when she's gone, but ya gotta do what ya gotta do, right? I'm Billie, by the way, Tosh's best friend, older sister, country mama, whatever. Where is that girl?"

She didn't know. And I had to tell her.

"Why don't we go sit in the living room?" I said.

She could sense it in my tone. "What the fuck's up?"

"Let's sit."

I led her into the living room and we both sat on the couch.

"Billie, I have some sad news."

Her mouth opened, her head cocked. "What kinda sad news?"

"Very sad." I gave her a moment. "Natasha is dead."

Her expression froze, but tears welled in her eyes. "How?"

"She died up on Platte Clove, she fell off a cliff, right now they think it was an accident or that she may have killed herself."

"No fucking way she killed herself," she spit out. Then she went absolutely still, except for her face, which slowly dissolved into a tear-riven blob.

You have to let people cry, give them space, especially if you've known them for under a minute. But the vehemence of her instinctive outburst — "No fucking way she killed herself" — bolstered my suspicions.

After she'd cried for a while she got up, walked into Natasha's kitchen, blew her nose on a paper towel, opened the fridge, took out a bottle of beer, twisted it open, took a long swig, and said, "I knew she was in trouble, I just didn't know . . . *oh fuck!*" She started crying again but this time it was over pretty quickly. "That kid was my best friend since the day she moved up here."

"So you met her when she moved to Phoenicia?"

"Yeah, I'm a singer, too. Sorta. I used to be. You know, clubs around here. But I been waiting tables at Brio's for thirty years, she came in, I served her, it was instant, we clicked, she was easy to click with, what a sweet kid, but lonely, screwed up. She'd messed up big time in the city, you know, fucked up her career. She needed a friend. Who fuckin' doesn't?"

Billie walked into the living room, sat

across from me, ran a finger around the rim of the beer bottle, and a terrible heavy sadness descended on her — she suddenly looked older, and broken.

"We sang together a few times, you know, just around in Woodstock and stuff, but that was such a gift she gave me. To appear with Natasha Wolfson, I mean she had *CDs* and reviews from hot-shit critics and shit. She had a lotta life in her, that kid." This time the tears were quiet and slow.

"Billie?"

"Yeah?"

"Can I ask you something?"

"G'head."

"If she didn't kill herself, how do you think she died?"

"I think somebody killed her."

"Who would kill her, why?"

Billie's eyes narrowed again, she studied me for a moment, then said, "Pavel, that guy she's been seeing, he's fuckin' *weird.*" I sensed she was holding something back — I'd seen it a thousand times with clients: the pause, the tentative tone, evading eye contact. Maybe she wasn't lying, but she wasn't truthing either.

"Weird how?"

"Too quiet, like a fox, you don't know what's really going on."

"Where did she meet him?"

"You tell me and we'll both know."

"What's he like?"

"He's from Czechland or someplace like that, fuckin-a-gorgeous and working it big-time, but pretending he isn't, you know what I mean? He's catnip to the chicks, I mean look at Natasha, she was gone on him, it's that whole still-waters-run-deep thing, you look in those green eyes of his and it's like you're hypnotized."

"Do you know where he is?"

"He lives down in Stone Ridge, on some big estate owned by two crazy English ladies, he lives above the garage or some shit, one of them is in love with him, I never trusted him. Yeah, he's hot, but shifty, Natasha got her head turned."

I just let her words hang there. I flashed on the dominatrix garb in the closet.

"How was Natasha making a living these days?"

She downed the beer in a long swallow, went and got another one. Billie was hard, hard and soft, but mostly hard — you get kicked enough times, you get hard. The breezy Stevie Nicks who'd blown in here was a memory: she'd lost the friend who made her feel good about herself = more hard in her life.

"Her rich-ass parents weren't helping her, that's for sure. Those two are first-class creeps."

"You met them?"

"Yeah, they came up here once, they're oh-so-motherfuckin'-charming if you can overlook the bullshit oozing out of their ears. Tosh said her Mom was trying to help her, but then why didn't they just cut her a check so she could move the fuck out to LA? She had *contacts* out there, big-time like." She got quiet and something hardened around her mouth, the tears were over, she was already moving on to the next class at her personal school of hard knocks. "Poor Tosh. She's gone. . . . What's it to you, by the way?"

"I met her, I liked her."

"She was a great kid, wasn't she?"

I nodded.

She scrutinized me, as if for the first time. "You look like a really nice person. You're pretty, too. I always wished I had green eyes."

"Is there *anything* else you can tell me about Natasha's life?"

Her eyes went down, she bit her lower lip. Then she looked up at me, almost innocent, and said, "No."

ELEVEN

I tooled down 212 toward Sawyerville in a less than a great mood — I couldn't believe I was letting myself get sucked into another murder, or whatever it was. This was supposed to be *my* time, the years when I took it easy and pursued my long-ignored quasi-interest in things like painting, Asian history, joining a reading group, and just doing a whole lot of nothing. I did not want to get sucked into some swirling vortex of a lost girl, her narcissistic parents, shady boyfriend, kinky sex, and murder. No way, no how. I had paid my dues to the human race, my footprint was light, leave me be.

Then I heard a faint echo: Natasha's voice singing *Love by Any Other Name* . . . the kindness in her eyes — and the fear. It was that fear — combined with everything I'd learned about suicide during my psychotherapy training and practice — that made me think somebody killed her. I couldn't let that sit. I just couldn't.

I hit the accelerator.

I dropped into Abba's. George was sitting at the counter, wearing jodhpurs. He stood up and modeled them for me.

"It's a hot look, don't you think?" he said.

"It's a look."

"You know, Janet, you really are a wet dishrag in human form. You feel threatened by passion. Antonio is my lover and my life, his world is my world — I start my riding lessons today."

"Hey, that's great, where?"

He sat on his stool, took a sip of coffee and said casually, "Emerson elementary."

"You're starting your riding lessons at an elementary school? Do they have horses there?"

"You're so *literal.*"

"Well, you *do* need a horse to have a riding lesson, don't you?"

"I'm starting out on a playground horse because I suffer from severe *equinophobia!* I was profoundly traumatized by a horse as a child."

"I'm sorry, I didn't know that. What happened?"

"I'm trying to remember . . . but I'm sure it had something to do with my father's penis."

"How's the Van Wyck campaign going?"

"I spent an hour calling voters today. His wife, Alice, dropped into headquarters with a wicker basket of tea sandwiches and cookies, it was a bit *noblesse oblige,* but whatever. They were good."

Abba came out from the kitchen and joined us. I filled them both in on my day.

"Do you know anything about two English sisters who live down in Stone Ridge?" When it came to the Hudson Valley, Abba was a font of history, the latest news and the juiciest gossip.

"Oh sure, the Bump sisters, Octavia and Lavinia, I'd say they're fiftyish, from some fancy British family, *a lot* of money, their dad was a lord or a knight or something, maybe minor royalty. Apparently they're pretty strange, so strange that the family basically pays them to stay on this side of the pond."

"Have you met them?"

"Never have. They mostly stick to their estate, it's on Leggett Road, probably the fanciest address in the county."

"Do you know anything about some beautiful young man who lives on their property?"

"I don't, but it sounds interesting."

"It does *not,*" George said, "I haven't even

looked at another man since I met Antonio. Are you going to head down there, Janet? Because I am in the mood for a little drive."

"I may pay a courtesy visit. But it should probably be solo."

"Their estate is right next to Collier Denton," Abba said.

"That name sounds familiar."

"He's an old actor, was on some soap opera for like thirty years, he's retired now."

"Collier Denton is a mad old queen from hell," George tossed in.

"Not sure I would phrase it like that," Abba said. "But I catered a party for him a few years ago and he was pretty . . . *grand.* And cheap, *very* cheap. Anyway, he and the sisters have been feuding for years, and I mean *seriously* feuding, lawsuits, the police have been called, I think there may even have been an attempted murder charge."

"Interesting. And now Natasha's beautiful boyfriend is in the mix," I said. "Listen, I better get going, see you both later."

I stepped outside and there was Mad John — tiny, hirsute, insane, the town's resident river rat — wearing his usual Oliver Twist outfit and sweeping down the sidewalks of Sawyerville, one of his favorite hobbies, the civic-minded little lunatic.

"Hey, Mad John."

He gave me his big, tooth-challenged grin, dropped the broom and hugged me — fragrant fella. "I love Jan-Jan."

"How's things out on the river?" Mad John lived in the reeds down by the lighthouse and plied the Hudson on his handmade raft.

A cloud passed over his face and he looked down.

"What's wrong?"

"Some bad stuff on the river, on the island."

"What do you mean bad? And what island?"

"Goat Island, old Indian island, boneyard, sacred island."

"What's happening there?"

"Stealing from the dead. From the spirits. Beautiful things, sacred things. *Valuable* things. I try and protect the island, but they still come."

Mad John may have been mad, but he was rock-solid reliable.

"Who's doing it?"

"I don't know, but I'll find out and they will pay. The Indian gods are angry and I am their avenger!"

"Be careful, Mad John."

He was quiet for a moment and then suddenly his face broke into a huge grin and he started to jump up and down in place — his favorite expression of joy — and sing:

"Don't worry, be crazy!
Don't worry, be crazy!"

He stopped and thrust his face at mine, *"Like a fox!"*

TWELVE

I considered calling down to the Bump sisters, but I'd learned that a pop visit is much likelier to yield interesting information — people don't have time to slap their game face on. But there was a phone call I wanted to make first.

"Hello?" Josie's foster mom answered. Even her hello was wary.

"Hi, Roberta, it's Janet Petrocelli down in Sawyerville. Is Josie around?"

"She's doing her after-school chores."

"Well, could I possibly interrupt her to say a quick hello?"

"I don't like to interrupt her when she's doing her chores."

I made a note to buy Josie a cell.

"I'm sure you don't, but I'd much appreciate it."

There was a pause and then a begrudging, "Don't keep her long."

"Hi, Janet," Josie sounded strong, if not

exactly happy. I felt a pang of longing.

"Hey, my friend, how are you?"

There was a short pause. "Good." I could tell Roberta was nearby listening to every word. "I was mowing the lawn."

"My least favorite chore."

"It's very grounding."

I laughed.

"How's school?"

There was another pause. The Maldens had enrolled Josie in a parochial school (don't get me started). "School is good."

"Hey, why don't I come up on Saturday and take you out to lunch?"

"Hold on a second . . . Mrs. Malden, I'm going to go out to lunch with Janet on Saturday."

I heard Roberta Malden say, "We'll have to check with Father about that." I hate it when a grown woman calls her husband "Father." Dr. Freud, I presume.

"I'm coming up, Josie, I'll be there around noon."

"See you then."

I was supposed to go out to Zack's for dinner and I was looking forward to it, especially dessert — Zack à la mode. But Natasha came first. I called Zack's cell; he was a landscape "architect" — he'd earned some kind of certificate after a three-week course at Ulster Community College — on a job in Woodstock.

"Hey, baby-baby sweet-baby, how goes it?" Zack purred.

"Things are okay, how are you?"

"I'm at one with the universe, out here making love to a gorgeous row of daylilies I nicknamed 'Janet'."

Zack was such a sweet sincere sexy guy, but when he said things like that I always wished he was just a little bit ironic. Our relationship, after a little over a year, had plateaued. We still had great sex, which had been a big part of the deal from the beginning, but I wanted a little more, I don't know, depth or something. He was a what-you-see-is-what-you-get kind of guy, which is definitely preferable to a lying-sack-of-shit kind of guy like the Asshole (a.k.a. my former husband), but I sometimes wished there were some surprising little twists to his personality, some hidden nooks and crannies, maybe even a little cosmic sadness. I couldn't help comparing him to Chevrona Williams, who felt like she had all those things.

"Listen, I'm not sure I can make it tonight," I said.

"Oh baby, I got us a gorgeous free-range chicken right from the farm, with my own potatoes and peas. Why not?"

"I have to head down to Stone Ridge, not sure what time I'll be back."

"Does this have something to do with that dead girl you bought the jewelry from?"

"Maybe."

"What happened to your new simple life up in the country?"

"Good question."

THIRTEEN

I headed down county. Stone Ridge sits on a ridge at the western edge of the Shawangunk Mountains, a rocky vein that rises between the fertile Rondout Valley and the Hudson Valley. The Gunks are wicked popular with climbers who love to clamber up their overhanging rock faces using their bare hands — which sounds pretty much like my definition of a living nightmare. This is one of the richer corners of the county — long settled, it feels much more tame than up in the Catskills, with prosperous old farms, orchards, stone houses, winding driveways, lawns dotted with specimen trees. This was definitely Van Wyck country, his "Building a *New* New York" lawn signs were a lot more in evidence here than in the scruffier parts of the valley.

I turned down Leggett Road — pow! I could have been over on the tony east bank of the Hudson — big old estates, sweeping lawns, stables, this was *la crème de la* Ulster County. Abba had given me directions to the Bump sisters' spread and there it was: a massive old wood house set way back from the road; a large wooden sign at the entrance to the drive read "Bumpland." The drive was lined with tall oaks, I drove past lovely gardens and a graceful pond nestled into the gentle downslope of lawn. The whole effect was stately and understated, that is until I began to notice little leprechaun, elf, and gnome figures tucked around — they looked like they'd escaped en masse from a miniature golf course or maybe a mental hospital for psychotic dwarfs; I guess their smiles were meant to be friendly but they looked leering and malevolent to me.

At the bottom of the lawn there was a tall barbed-wire fence plastered with "No Trespassing" signs — on the other side sat Collier Denton's estate, his stone house not far from the property line, clearly too close for anyone's comfort. The fence was pretty jarring — a jolt of the South Bronx in Shangri-La.

As I approached the house, I saw there was a service road that branched off and led to a barn, other outbuildings, and a large two-story garage; Billie had told me that Pavel lived above the garage. I parked, climbed the portico of the big house, and knocked on the front door. A middle-aged Hispanic woman in a maid's uniform answered — her challenging expression and the cigarette dangling from her left hand were a warm welcome.

"Hi, I'm here to see Octavia or Lavinia Bump."

"Who is it?" a fruity English voice called from somewhere inside the house.

"Some person, I don't know," the maid called back.

"Oh, how divine, a *person,* and they're just in time for tea!" A rather large woman sailed into the foyer. I pegged her for mid-fifties, with a round pretty face, milky skin, unruly red (dye-pot) hair, large green eyes; she was full-figured to say the least and carried it with great aplomb in a thigh-high low-cut dress that showed off her shapely legs and ample bosom; the deep red lipstick was the coup de grace — this gal radiated a distracted but highly sexed energy. She clasped her hands together in front of her chest, thrilled to have company. "Hello, how do you do? I'm Octavia Bump."

"Hi, it's a pleasure, I'm Janet Petrocelli."

"How marvelous — Petrocelli! I adore Italy! I had one of my first great love affairs in Siena, during Il Palio, his name was

Maurizio — oh, the places he took me, all without leaving his bed. Mummy and Daddy were *livid,* so silly of them, I was a very mature fourteen!" She turned to the maid, "Would you be a dear girl and set another place for tea, Inez."

"I'm Maria."

"Oh dear, so sorry." She turned to me, "I've just met a maid named Maria." She pealed with laughter and took my hand. "After tea, we'll read Dante — 'Midway along the pathway . . .' "

Octavia led me through a series of gorgeous old rooms that looked like no one ever set foot in them; they were furnished in Early Balmoral, lots of chintz-covered sofas, graceful moldings, wood paneling, Persian rugs — the sole discordant note was the array of Jackson-Pollocky-without-the-talent paintings that adorned all the walls. As we passed from room to room, I saw several maids dart out of eyeshot.

We reached an immense sunroom in which an immense table was set for an immense tea — cakes and cookies and puddings and pies and bars and trifles — and one tiny plate of crustless sandwiches for any diabetics who might drop in.

"Do make yourself at home, my darling *amica Italiana!*" Octavia sat down, took a plate and started to heap it with goodies. "I had a mad affair in Capri when I was fifteen, his name was Angelo and he was so roughhewn, primordial, it was like being ravaged by a Neanderthal. Mummy and Daddy were livid *again,* which I thought was terribly narrow-minded of them, just because Angelo was a peasant, I mean he *owned* his donkey, and reading is such an overrated skill, don't you agree?"

"I've actually never been to Italy, and my mother was Jewish."

"Was she? How *marvelous.*" She took a big bite of orange-frosted cake. "When I was fifteen I almost eloped with an Israeli soldier — after we made mad love, Ari would read to me from the Torah, in Hebrew, it was divinely incomprehensible, I wanted to buy a kibbutz and have his babies. Need I tell you Mummy and Daddy were livid." She turned to a maid who was slouching in the doorway. "Juanita dear, do bring the tea! . . . Unless you'd rather gin?"

"Tea is fine."

The maid left. Octavia took a huge mouthful of some greenish pudding. "I must warn you that my sister Lavinia will be appearing at any moment. Of course I adore her, but she is . . ." she leaned in close and lowered her voice, *". . . peculiar."*

"Is she?"

"Oh yes." She popped a cookie in her mouth. "It happened when Daddy died, she quite lost the plot, now she spends all day with Jerome. I'm quite fond of Jerome, but at a certain age one must *refresh* oneself. That's why I took up painting, it's released *all* my inhibitions." She gestured vaguely to the huge splattered canvases. "A curator from Vassar came over and pronounced my work *arresting.* Would you like to know my secret?"

I nodded.

"I paint from my vagina. I just pretend that I've chopped my head right off and my id pours onto the canvas like a *cosmic orgasm!* My dear, you haven't touched a crumb."

Juanita/Inez/Maria appeared with a large silver teapot. "Thank you, Lupe." Octavia poured us both tea; it was strong enough to peel paint.

"I wanted to ask you about your boarder, Pavel."

Octavia's whole demeanor changed, she sat up straight and eyeballed me. "Pavel has been *very* naughty."

"Oh?"

"He's been spending time with that *other woman,* that crass little nobody who lives up in the woods somewhere."

"You mean Natas—"

She clasped her hands over her ears and cried, *"Don't mention that name in my presence!"* She lowered her hands to her lap in a great show of restoring her dignity. "What you have to understand is that Pavel is the great love of my life. And I of his. He has proposed marriage to me. I, of course, as a lady must, have withheld my consent — I have a duty to uphold my family's standards. And so to punish me, he's undertaken this meaningless dalliance with that tawdry mountain woman. I've heard she has *enormous feet!*"

"Natasha Wolfson is dead."

Octavia's eyes went wide and her mouth dropped open. Then she was still for a long suspended moment. "Are you quite sure? *Dead?*"

I nodded.

She stood up and began to pace, a flush of triumph racing up her bosom to her face. "Does Pavel know?"

"I don't know."

"I must go find him!" She raced halfway out of the room, turned, came over and lightly cupped my face in her hands, her eyes welled, "You're my angel, my Italian-Jewish angel, sent from the heavens or Tel

Aviv or wherever . . ." A half-mad smile spread across her face. "*Do* have some gooseberry pudding!"

Off she sped.

I tried the gooseberry pudding — boy, that is some weird-ass food, slimy and sour, like something they'd make you eat on a reality show. A maid walked by the doorway, texting. I looked out the picture window at Collier Denton's estate on the other side of the barbwire fence. His house was a rambling old stone affair, the kind second-homers swoon over, surrounded by some serious gardens that had gone a bit to seed, when you looked closely the paint on the house was worn and chipped. A high cloud passed over the sun and suddenly the day grew dark and the scene looked forlorn and melancholy.

"Ripping good tea here, Jerome."

I turned to see a mannish woman (she would have been a mannish man, too) walk into the room; her build was similar to her sister's but she was wearing a tweed jacket, oxford shirt, tie, wool slacks, and men's shoes, all of it a bit disheveled and not altogether clean. Her short hair was slicked back but had burst loose in a few places, and there was a small identically dressed stuffed monkey perched on her left shoulder. She saw me and stuck out a hand.

"Vin Bump, how are you?"

"Janet Petrocelli, nice to meet you."

"This is Jerome."

"Hi, Jerome."

"He's a bit out of sorts today, his fibromyalgia is acting up. Where's that sister of mine?"

"She went looking for Pavel."

"I don't trust that lad!"

"No?"

"He's cast some sort of spell on my sister. Not the first, believe me. She's been led through life by her pudenda. I love her dearly but you do know she's . . ." she leaned toward me and lowered her voice, *". . . unstable."*

"Is she?"

"Absolute nutter! It all started when she was born — being a female is a wretched fate. My condolences to you on that account, dear girl. Believe me, I thank Jupiter every day for my dangly-bits. Time for tea, Jerome." Vin took out a flask and filled a teacup full of whiskey, then poured in a single drop of tea and took a long swallow. "It's a bloody marvelous Assam, isn't it?"

"It's nice and strong."

"Esmerelda, Jerome would like a steak and kidney pie," Vin called in the direction of the kitchen. "I can't abide steak and kidney pie myself, but Jerome loves it."

A maid brought in a steak and kidney pie, still in its tin but with the lid off. As she put it on the table, Lavinia reached out and pinched her bohunkus.

"Jerome, stop that! Terribly sorry, Selena, he's in a mood, his fibromyalgia."

The maid nonchalantly picked up a lemon square and walked out.

Vin cut herself a big slice of the steak and kidney pie and began to devour it. "I do hope Pavel isn't down at Denton's, that always drives Octavia right round the bend."

"Oh?"

"Oh, good God, yes. Those two bonkers are both mad for the lad, have come to blows on more than one occasion. Jerome has tried to intercede, but they've no interest in making peace."

As if on cue, we watched through the picture window as a Mercedes plowed down Collier Denton's drive and skidded to a stop in front of his house. Octavia leapt out of the car, ran to the front door and banged on it.

"Oh my, there she goes!" Vin said, not making much effort to disguise her excitement.

The door opened and a tall elderly man

in a silk dressing gown stepped out.

"That's Denton, I do hope neither of them is armed!" Vin chortled.

Octavia asked Denton something, he shook his head and turned away from her, she grabbed his shoulder and spun him around, he slapped her, she slapped him back. He raised an arm and ordered her off his property. She planted her feet and crossed her arms over her chest. He took out a cell phone and started to punch in a number. She turned and stormed over to her car, got in, and roared off, spitting gravel. Denton put away the phone, straightened up and walked back into his house.

Vin clucked in disappointment, "That was lovely-jubbly compared to their real rows." Then she helped herself to a second piece of steak and kidney pie, "Jerome's fibromyalgia always gives him an appetite."

"And it's all over Pavel?"

"Precisely. Denton is a poofter, don't you know. I don't care a fidget as long as he keeps his bloody hands off my arse!"

I'd treated clients with gender-identity issues and was in awe of how well Lavinia had resolved hers; her personality-displacement psychosis was another matter.

But it was time for me to get moving — I needed to find this Pavel.

FOURTEEN

Just as I left the house, Octavia pulled up and leapt out of her car. "I'm afraid I shall have to *kill* that dreadful man. But never mind, he's just jealous. The witch is dead, I've won, Pavel is *mine!!* Ciao-shalom, dear girl, no time to chat, must go paint, my vagina is *adamant!*"

She raced into the house in a fit of . . . Octavianess.

I got in my car but instead of heading down the drive, I turned up the service road and parked behind the garage, out of sight of the main house. I got out and ducked into the garage.

Inside were a dusty Bentley, a Jaguar, and a Land Rover; there were also ancient croquet sets, tennis rackets, saddles, and the like. Clearly these gals didn't get out of their hothouse too often, and they also clearly had more money than they knew what to do with.

I climbed a staircase at the back of the garage and opened the door into a large loft-like room with a peaked ceiling. It had unpainted wood walls, a vintage kitchen at one end, a woodstove, simple windows, and was furnished in a minimal masculine way, with an enormous roughhewn table, an iron-frame bed, Mission-style chairs, a few bleached animal skulls, a Navajo blanket, wooden candlesticks — the effect was kind of macho chic, like a magazine spread on the weekend house of two gay guys who work in fashion.

There was a picture of Natasha on the refrigerator door and several of her CDs were on the table, along with a small pile of maps of the Hudson Valley, including a nautical map of the river; a bunch of vitamin and supplement bottles were on the kitchen counter. Otherwise the place was without much character, I couldn't get any real sense of who Pavel was, except maybe a certain primal simplicity — or the pretense of same.

I was about to head into the bathroom when I heard the sounds of an approaching motorcycle. I looked out a window — the bike pulled to a stop near my car, the rider swung his long leg over the machine and pulled off his helmet, took a step toward my car and eyed it. Then he walked into the garage.

I tried to compose myself as his footfalls echoed up the stairs. He got to the top, saw me, and stopped. Then he smiled, a slightly lopsided smile, the power of which he was well aware.

Yes, Pavel lived up to his billing — tall, lean and muscled, with a hank of the thickest brown hair on the planet, tawny skin, a killer jawline, a full mouth, and green eyes that just pulled you in, soulful and full of some ineffable promise — a better world, maybe? Or was it just the best sex in history? Stunning as the parts were, the whole was greater, it was his grace, aura, the off-kilter smile — and he was just so *hot.* Beauty and sex appeal are two different qualities — I had clients no one would call pretty who spent their lives fighting off advances, and great-looking clients who had a hard time getting laid — Pavel was the ultimate fusion of the two.

Yup, the Gods had smiled on this dude; he had landed at Bumpland and might very well become lord of the manor — clearly those green eyes were not as guileless as they seemed. I reminded myself that the Gods are fickle.

"Hi," he said.

"I assume you're Pavel."

"That is me." He had a pretty strong Eastern European accent.

"I'm Janet Petrocelli."

"Hello, Janet Petrocelli."

"You're probably wondering what I'm doing in your house?"

He shrugged. Clearly he was used to people showing up at his house, wherever he lived.

"I'm a friend of Natasha," I said, ready to clock his reaction.

He smiled again. "I cannot reach Natasha. Did she send you to give me a message?"

If he was acting, he was doing a pretty good job. Either way, the next step was to tell him — and keep an eagle eye on his response.

"No, she didn't send me. I came on my own." I moved toward him. "Pavel, I have some sad news about her."

He cocked his head, quizzical.

"She's dead."

His face grew very grave. "Natasha is dead?"

"Yes."

He stood dead still for a moment, before asking, "How did she die?"

"It's unclear."

"Where did she die?"

"On top of Platte Clove. She either fell, jumped, or was pushed from a cliff."

He went into the kitchen, opened a cabinet, took out a bottle of vodka, poured himself a glass. He downed it in one swallow, clenched his jaw. Then he hurled the glass across the room, where it shattered against a wall. We stood in silence. He went to the large table and lit a candle, then he put on one of Natasha's CDs. Her voice filled the room, he smiled at me, sad and sweet, his eyes filled with tears. If this was acting, he was good at it.

"I cannot believe this," he said.

"How long have you known her?" I asked.

"For a few months. She is a very special woman. . . . Now she is gone."

"When did you last see her?"

"Friday night."

I waited for him to say more, knowing from my years in practice that many people felt a need to fill a silence, and the words that gushed out were often deeply revealing. Pavel felt no such need.

"How did she seem on Friday night?" I asked.

"Beautiful. We went for a night walk and then made love."

"She didn't seem . . . frightened at all?"

"She had much on her mind, she was a

complicated woman, she kept a part of herself secret from me. She wanted to move to Los Angeles, I wanted her to stay."

"Haven't you proposed to Octavia?"

"You ask a lot of questions."

"I'm the curious type."

"Sometimes it is better not to know. Keeps you out of trouble."

"Did you meet Natasha's family?"

"One time. At a party at her parents' house."

"And?"

"It made Natasha very angry."

"Did something happen?"

His cellphone rang; he looked at the incoming number and didn't answer. "Natasha is dead and all you do is ask more questions." He moved to the top of the stairs. "I need to be alone now."

"I'm sure we'll meet again," I said as I passed him on my way out.

FIFTEEN

My trip to Stone Ridge had yielded more questions than answers and my mind was clenched and swirling at the same time. I couldn't really get a bead on Pavel, he didn't seem particularly surprised that Natasha was dead, but at the same time throwing that glass seemed like an act of spontaneous rage at the world. Was he devious or just playing the only card he had? As for Octavia, how far could her passion and jealousy have taken her? I needed a little stress-reducing recreation — thankfully it was still early enough to get up to Zack's.

I sped up to West Sawyerville, where Zack's dollhouse of a cabin sat beside the rushing Plattekill, hard under the eastern escarpment of the Catskills. I found him out in the yard puttering around, as per usual; wearing nothing but crocs and a pair of funky cargo shorts, also as per usual. Every time I saw Zack in this almost-naked state my heart went pitter-pat (okay, it wasn't my heart).

"There she is, my little darlin', prettiest flower in all the garden. You look tired, baby girl. Here, have a sip, this will fix you right up."

He handed me his Zackwacker, which was basically a whole lot of tequila blendered up with whatever fresh (or frozen) (or canned) fruit he had in the kitchen. It was a delicious and wickedly potent concoction, and it went down easy, especially tonight. I sat on one of the bluestone benches he'd built around the property and looked up at the mountains, glowing in the twilight. In theory this was one of those mellow moments I'd moved upstate to savor, my new laid-back life. In reality my little internal combustion engine was firing on all pistons and the hum sounded a lot like *Natasha-Natasha-Natasha.*

We went inside and while he cooked, I sat at the kitchen table and filled him in on my day down in Stone Ridge.

"I know that Collier Denton character; my old company did his gardens." Before he earned his landscaping "degree" and went out on his own, Zack worked for a big local landscaper.

"No kidding, what was he like?"

"Dude put the sleaze in sleazy, always had these hustler types hanging around. Plus he stiffed my boss for something like five grand."

"He just didn't pay it?"

"Bingo. He lived like royalty — a queen to be exact. You should have heard him, 'I'm sorry, my dear boy, but that hydrangea plant simply *must* be moved three inches to the left.' And this is at 9 in the a.m. while he's drinking a glass of champagne. Then he got fired from his soap opera gig for showing up drunk, and then he started selling shit from his house; he had all kinds of paintings and silver and knick-knacks and stuff, the place was like a museum. He also switched to Champale for breakfast. Then he stopped paying his bills, there were all sorts of excuses. Finally we just quit."

"What about those hustlers?"

"They were hot kids, I remember one was Dominican, another was a hick from up in Schoharie County. Denton would always be trying to 'educate' them, reciting Shakespeare and playing operas, but you could tell he was nothing but a meal ticket to them — and under his mentor schtick, they were nothing but sex toys to him. There was always some kind of blowup after a month or two and he'd kick them out."

Was Pavel his latest hustler? And if Denton was as obsessed with Pavel as Octavia was, well, who knows what dark corners of the soul it could have led him into.

"I need to meet this guy."

"He's a sucker for fans and flattery, old ladies used to show up at his house with presents, he creamed every time, invited them in, showed off the place. I'm telling you, he's a total freak."

I could feel my adrenaline kick up a notch, my short hairs tingle, my throat tighten. The truth is pathology excites me, the swirling vortex of lust/obsession/degeneracy/evil, the question of how far a human being will go — and what it is within us that *allows* us to go that far. I took a deep sip of the Zackwacker.

Zack leaned over and opened the oven door to braise the chicken. His shorts rode low and pulled tight against his firm beefy butt.

"Close that oven door," I said.

He straightened and turned to me, "Wassup?"

I walked over to him and undid the top button of his shorts.

"I'm in an eat-dessert-first mood."

SIXTEEN

I sat at my kitchen table the next morning reading a follow-up story on Natasha's death in the *Freeman.* The investigation had turned up no signs of foul play, although the cause of death was still officially listed as "undetermined"; it also stated that a memorial service was going to be held in Cold Spring on Saturday evening.

I was sure that Natasha's friend Billie up in Phoenicia was holding out on me. I called her.

"It's Janet Petrocelli."

"Oh, hi." She sounded wary.

"How are you?"

"I'm okay."

"Are you going to Natasha's memorial?"

There was a pause. "I can't, I can't handle it."

"Listen, I'd like to talk."

"What about?"

"Natasha."

"I just lost my best friend and I'm not doing that well."

"I want to find out what really happened with her death."

"Thinking about it, maybe she did kill herself. She wasn't happy."

"If every unhappy person killed themselves, the world would be a ghost town." I heard her light a cigarette and take a deep pull. "What do you say? Let me buy you a drink."

There was a long pause, then, "Okay, but nowhere around here." I heard fear.

"Name your spot."

She took another deep pull on her smoke and said, "New Paltz."

"You got it. Does tonight work for you?"

"Yeah."

I hung up, went into my office/storeroom and went online to find Collier Denton's phone number. I basically hate going online — the whole world is suddenly at your fingertips. I can barely handle the ten feet in front of me, the last thing I want is the whole goddamn world. Shopping online is a freakout. I once went looking for kitchen drawer pulls and with each click I found myself sucked further into a special rung of cyberhell populated by ten trillion kitchen drawer pulls — and each pull could be *enlarged* and viewed from different angles. I ended up — my head one pull away from exploding — ordering these absurd undulating purple-and-orange striped pulls, and when they arrived I was so ashamed that I left them on the front stoop of the animal shelter thrift shop after dark.

But finding a phone number I could handle. And Denton was listed. While pop visits were my preferred M.O., I wanted to be sure I wouldn't be greeted by a slammed door. After all, judging from his response to Octavia he was in a pretty foul head these days.

"Yes?" the affected baritone drawled.

"Hi, is this the Collier Denton who was the star of *The Well Runs Deep*?"

" 'Tis he indeed."

"Hi, my name is Janet Petrocelli, I moved upstate about a year ago and when I heard you were local, well, it would just be an utter thrill for me to meet you."

I didn't mention that I'd never seen his show, that watching even ten seconds of a soap opera plunged me into existential despair — I always associated them with childhood sick days spent on an itchy couch in the gloomy den of whatever boozy beaten-down relative was currently putting me up. And that ominous music: Melodies to Commit Suicide By.

"Well, I'm *awfully* busy weighing offers and reading scripts, but I suppose that could be arranged. What time could you get here?"

"How about two o'clock?"

"Let me check my datebook . . . *hmmmm* . . . yes, two works. I have some time between my Flemish lesson and my harpsichord recital."

"You speak Flemish and play the harpsichord?"

"The truth is immensely overrated. Do you know how to find *Fleur de Moi?*"

"Sure do. See you at two."

"Oh, one thing."

"Yes."

"I have a special fondness for Veuve Clicquot."

Just as I hung up, someone rang the doorbell down in the shop. I went down to find George and Mad John outside.

"Come in, guys, what's up?"

Mad John made a beeline for Bub, who adored him. They started up an animated coo-and-caw which a jealous Sputnik — he found Mad John delightfully smellworthy — interrupted with some fierce nuzzling.

George was still wearing jodhpurs. "We need your help with Goat Island," he said.

"What can I do?"

"We want to catch the looters. That island was sacred to the Esopus Indians for thousands of years. It could turn out to be a major archeological site and these creeps are tearing it up."

"When the bad people dig up the magic relics, they release demons, demons that haunt us all and make bad things happen on the river and in the valley," Mad John said. Then he started jumping up and down in place, "Gotta stop it, gotta stop it!"

"Isn't that the state's job?"

"There's no money for things like that these days," George said. "*We* have to do it." When he got passionate about saving the valley I was reminded of why I loved him.

"How?"

"Mad John has been casing the island regularly and it seems like the looting is happening in the middle of the night. He thinks we should all go over there and spend a night waiting for the thieves."

"Could that be dangerous?"

Mad John made a gargoyle face and said, "The demons are dangerous."

I took a deep breath. Spending a night on a deserted island in the middle of the Hudson waiting for potentially armed thieves to arrive sounded . . . well, I guess when I thought about it, it sounded kind of exciting.

"Yeah, sure, I'll do it."

Mad John leapt up, wrapped himself around me and cried, "I love Jan-Jan!"

This drove Sputnik into a paroxysm of jealousy and he leapt up and threw himself against me, causing all of us to tumble into a heap on a nearby sofa.

"Will you please grow up?" George huffed.

"No," Mad John said.

"Still wearing the jodhpurs?" I asked.

"I've just come from my riding lesson, Antonio says I'm making incredible progress."

"On a playground horse?"

"I hate to disappoint you, Janet, but I've graduated from the playground horse."

"That's great, so you're on a real horse now?"

"Sort of, yes."

"What do you mean sort of?"

"The horse I am now training on resembles a real horse in many important ways, it's an enormous step up in difficulty from the playground horse. It *bucks.*"

"It bucks?"

"Yes, darling, it bucks."

"Wait . . . it's not the mechanical horse

over at Price Chopper, is it?"

"Maybe."

I bit my tongue — the image of George getting a riding lesson on a kiddie horse in front of the supermarket was just too much.

"You know, Janet, the look on your face right now says it all. Well, it's very easy to mock innocence and passion, but Antonio and I are in love and don't care what the world thinks. In fact, I may move to the pampas with him, then you'll be sorry."

"When do we get to meet him?"

"Antonio comes from a very macho culture."

"Yes?"

"Which is why he's not gay."

"He's not gay?"

"He's not *gay* gay."

"Okay."

"But we're not hung up on labels."

"How old is he?"

"Okay, I'm not going down this road."

"He young! He young! He young!" Mad John cried, jumping up and down again.

George puffed up and said, "He's an old soul."

"He young!"

"This discussion is over. We're going over to the island next Thursday, we'll rendezvous at Mad John's at sunset. I am now leaving, with my dignity intact." He marched to the door, opened it, then stopped short and turned, "Oh, Janet, do you have any spare quarters, I want to go practice my canter."

Seventeen

I picked up a chilled bottle of Veuve Clicquot to ensure my welcome and hopefully loosen Collier Denton's lips. I headed down to Stone Ridge through the Rondout Valley, always a fun drive because the landscape is so flat and agricultural with miles of vegetable and corn fields, rambling farmhouses, popular farmstands; this Rondout Creek bottomland is some of the richest soil in the northeast and driving through you can smell the dense crumbly loam and imagine the first Dutch settlers claiming its bounty, building their stone houses, filled with promise and hope and industry. What would they make of the Olive Gardens and crack dens?

I drove past Bumpland and turned at the faded wooden sign reading *Fleur de Moi.* Signs of neglect were everywhere — the pond looked silty, the lawns patchy, the gardens overgrown, the house chipped and a bit sad. The whole place was romantic and evocative in an old-alcoholic-with-dwindling-funds-lives-within kind of way.

As I parked, I saw a curtain pulled back, a face in the shadows. I got out and as I approached the house, the front door flew open to reveal Collier Denton.

"Hello, my dear," he oozed, his eyes going right to the bottle. Wearing the same silk dressing gown I'd seen him in the other day, he was tall, thin, stood erect, was still handsome in an ancient way, with a strong jaw, deep-set eyes, and plenty of wavy silver hair. But there was something ghoulish going on here, a sense of dissolution and depravity in the hollow cheeks, hooded eyes, and ripe mouth.

"I brought you a little present," I said, holding up the bottle of bubbly.

He snatched it from my hand. "*Do* come in." He was all tattered grace-and-charm as he ushered me into the large, low rambling manse. "I'll fetch a flute," he said, leading me through a series of dusty rooms that looked three-quarters furnished; there were empty spaces on the walls where pictures had once hung, furniture was missing, in one room the floor was covered with a large pad but no rug.

We ended up in a wood-paneled library

off a messy kitchen that looked like it hadn't seen a fruit or vegetable in decades — I noticed sardine tins, jars of olives, and an industrial-size package of Pecan Sandies.

The library was dominated by a fireplace with a massive portrait of one Collier Denton hanging over it — dashing and debonair and forty years younger. A large armchair sat in one corner, clutter radiated out from it in concentric circles; clearly this was where Denton spent most of his waking hours. He crossed the room and shut the lid on the laptop that sat on a TV tray next to his chair, but not before I got a glimpse of porno. Then he headed over to a liquor cart before turning to me and asking, with mock graciousness, as if the thought had just occurred to him, "Oh, did *you* want any champagne?"

"I'm fine, thanks."

He didn't even attempt to disguise his relief. He grabbed a flute, sat in his armchair, deftly popped open the Veuve, tipped his flute and poured himself a glass. Drug of choice safely in hand, he snuggled into his chair, took a long sip and gave a little shudder of delight. Up close, he looked mottled and rheumy; I pegged him on the far shore of eighty. When the sleeve of his dressing gown rode up, I noticed a long burn scar on the inside of his left forearm that was haphazardly covered in thick pancake make-up.

"So I suspect you were madly in love with me in a father-figurey sort of way," he said, setting himself up for a fuselage of flattery.

"I'm not sure *I* was in love with you, but I'm sure a lot of women were."

"The network had to hire a secretary to handle my fan mail. I received an average of forty marriage proposals a week. One poor creature threw herself into the Mississippi clutching my photograph," he said, sounding delighted at the thought. "And the panties! Good lord, they came in by the score. Fortunately some of them were my size." He roared with laughter and poured himself another glass of champagne. "I suppose you'll want an autographed photo. I'm *awfully* busy weighing offers and reading scripts, but I suppose that could be arranged. They're twenty dollars, two for thirty, they make *marvelous* Christmas gifts and party favors."

I noticed a pharmacy bag next to his laptop and wondered what mad combination of meds he was on. From the way he was merrily prattling on, I suspected a happy pill (or two) was in the mix.

"Did you know I've donated my archives

to Lincoln Center? It was *wrenching* to part with it all, but a tax deduction is a tax deduction so I shipped them off six months ago. I just stuffed everything in an enormous packing crate and called UPS, I didn't bother *organizing* it — I'm sure there are bookish little fairies down there who *live* for that kind of thing, I mean it's a *national treasure* — I did summer stock with Robert Goulet *and* Sandy Duncan! I'm sure Lincoln Center will send an acknowledgment when they're done sorting through it all. Of course, it's just the *tip* of the iceberg, publishers are *clamoring* for my memoirs but I'm far too discreet, I mean I've slept with *everyone;* Sal Mineo *threw* himself at me. I threw him back."

He roared with more laughter and poured himself another flute full. The bottle was half gone and I didn't want to be around for the crash, plus the lips were definitely loosed. Time to make my move.

"I'm inhaling all this, Collier, but I'm actually here to talk about something else."

His head jerked and his eyes opened wide, like he'd been slapped. "Something *else?* Besides *me?*"

"You're part of it."

"Well, I should hope so. You're in *my* house, after all." He turned away from me and stage whispered to an imaginary friend, "Manners have gone *right* out the window."

"I wanted to talk about Pavel."

His head swung back with such alacrity that I was afraid it was going to keep going and spin all the way around, Exorcist-style. He puffed up in his chair, shot me an acid look, and intoned: *"What. About. Pavel?"*

"Did you know his girlfriend died last week?"

"Do I look like I live under a rock?"

I bit my tongue.

"I think she may have been murdered."

"Really? If you find the killer's address do let me know, I'm a great believer in thank-you notes."

"Will do."

"It was probably one of the Remittance Sisters," he said, gesturing in the direction of the Bump estate.

"You mean Octavia Bump?"

He shuddered. "She of porcine mien and manner, yes."

"Do you really think she's capable of murder?"

"She was capable of stealing Pavel from me, she's capable of anything. Don't be fooled by her tawdry little quivery ditz act, she has a *steeltrap* mind — not to mention other regions."

"She stole Pavel from you?"

"Young lady, I *discovered* Pavel. In the slums of Prague . . . well, it was a hotel bar but never mind, he *came* from the slums. I cleaned him up and brought him to this country, I invested time, money, and . . ." he placed a hand on his chest and his voice grew soft and fraught, *". . . my heart."*

Ham *and* cheese.

Then he switched gears, poured the last of the champagne as a veil of cunning descended over his eyes. "I'm afraid Lady Bump shall soon discover she's living in a fool's paradise."

"Oh?"

He downed the last drop of bubbly. "Now-now, do *I* look like a fool? I don't know who you are, or why you're here, but your audience is over."

He stood and ushered me out of the library and into the kitchen — there was a young man at the far end of the room, wearing black Levis and tee-shirt — pale and muscular, sexy and furtive. Denton looked annoyed at his presence.

"Oh, this is Graham," he said. "He's a handyman, doing some work for me."

" 'ello," Graham mumbled in a thick Irish accent.

"Let me show you out," Denton said,

grabbing my elbow and giving me a firm tug.

EIGHTEEN

New Paltz, which sits in the flats of the Hudson Valley, is one of those college towns that seems to hover under its own personal cloud of pot smoke. We're talking funky here — coffee shops, taco stands, bookstores, bars, used clothing shops, hippies of all ages — it's Woodstock's rowdier kid sister, the one who's still dropping acid and giving head in the stacks.

Feeling very middle-aged (and thankful for it), I parked and headed for the bar where I'd agreed to meet Billie. It was a dark spot on a side street that clearly catered more to townies and bikers than college kids. I didn't see her so I got a ginger ale at the bar, sat at a small table, and waited. The place was pretty crowded and had a sweaty vibe, rough around the edges, vintage Aerosmith was playing, there was a pool table, the knot of jumpy lowlifes pow-wowing in one corner screamed *we-love-our-meth.*

Then Billie walked in. It took me a minute to realize it was her — Stevie Nicks was long gone, replaced by Amy Winehouse's favorite aunt. She had on a teased-up black wig that was slightly askew, sunglasses, a too-tight spangly purple top, a black leather miniskirt, and clunky high heels. There isn't a woman in the world who could carry off this look (well, maybe a few truck-stop hookers) and at Billie's age, it was just sad. She rushed over to my table.

"Hi, hon," she gushed, looking over her shoulder at the entrance to the bar, as if to check if she was being followed.

"Hi, Billie, how are you?"

"Kinda ragged 'round the edges."

"I'm sorry to hear it."

"Natasha's death hit me like a fucking runaway truck. I'm gettin' outta here."

"Where are you going?"

"Florida. I got a girlfriend in Jacksonville, she's gonna put me up for a while." She took off the sunglasses and her eyes were puffy and bloodshot and anxious.

A gnarly oldtimer at the bar was looking at us. Billie noticed him and crossed her legs.

"Can I be honest with you, Billie?"

"I'm always real, no bullshit."

"The other day, when I asked you if there

was anything about Natasha's life that I should know, I got the feeling you were being evasive."

Her mouth quivered and she said, "I need a drink."

"Let me get it."

"Triple tequila straight and a Heineken."

I walked up to the bar and ordered. The gnarly guy smiled at me — it's nice to know that not *everyone* is obsessed with the condition of their teeth — and I returned a discouraging little nod.

I brought Billie's booze back to the table and she downed the tequila in one long swallow. "I fuckin' love tequila," she said before chugging her brew. She looked over at the gnarly guy.

"So, about Natasha . . ."

"Alright, I'm going to lay it out. It's my fucking fault she's dead. How you think that feels?"

I shrugged.

"I feel like a worthless piece of shit, but she needed work, she needed to make some money. I didn't tell her at first, I didn't tell her for months. Then I told her."

"Told her what?"

"Can you get me another, hon?"

I went to the bar and got her another tequila, ignoring the gnarly guy whose smile was tilting toward a leer.

"So what did you tell her?"

"Where she could find work."

"And where was that?"

She downed the tequila. Her eyes welled with tears. "I never should have fuckin' told her."

"Billie, I'm trying to find out who murdered her. I need your help."

"I sent her to Kelly's Farm."

"What's Kelly's Farm?"

"What, do I need to spell it out for you — Kelly's Farm is a whorehouse."

"Okay."

"For men who like it kinky."

"Where is it?"

"It's way deep up in the motherfuckin' Catskills."

"Can you be a little more specific?"

"It's up past Delhi, in some beyond-fuckall valley."

"So she was working there, why would that lead to her murder?"

"*A lot* of big shots go to Kelly's Farm."

"Okay."

"She didn't tell me his name, but she said she had a client who was big time, like serious big time. In politics. Married, kids. Put it together: he wants to be governor or some shit. But he's got a little secret that could slam the brakes on that wet dream pretty fuckin' fast."

"Thanks for telling me this."

"Like I said: I'm real."

She was looped and must have forgotten she was wearing a wig because she ran her fingers through her hair and shook her head, sending the wig even more akimbo. Then she looked over at the gnarly guy and turned sideways so that one butt cheek lifted off her chair and her miniskirt rode up so high that she was dealing crack. The gnarly guy smiled and rearranged his junk. It's always fun to observe native mating rituals, but I had promises to keep.

I stood up, "Listen, Billie, please keep in touch."

"Yeah sure," she said vaguely.

By the time I got to the door the lovebirds were making out at the table.

NINETEEN

It was Saturday. Natasha's memorial was in the evening, down in Cold Spring, and I was taking Josie out to lunch up in Troy. It all added up to a lot of driving, but no way was I going to miss either one.

The day was windy with high skittering clouds. I like speeding up the Thruway through the lush hills, paradoxically it slows my mind down, lets me get some decent thinking done. I ran through what I knew about Natasha's death. Certainly Octavia Bump and Collier Denton were glad she was out of the way. And I sure as hell didn't trust Pavel. Then there was Kelly's Farm, which opened up a whole new box of worms. I stuck in my earpiece and called Abba.

"Do you know anything about a brothel up in Delaware County that caters to the more esoteric erotic pursuits?" I asked her.

"Rings a vague bell. Why?"

"Natasha Wolfson worked there. Apparently one of her clients was a powerful politician."

"Interesting. Let me make a few calls."

I reached Albany and kept going. This was my first visit to see Josie since she'd moved to Troy and I was more than a little nervous. I had to face up to the fact that she'd rekindled something in me that had been long dormant — my maternal instincts. They'd been dormant for a couple of reasons. First of all my nature, I'm just not a particularly maternal type, I never had that overpowering urge or need to have a mini-me around. Then there was my (non-) experience with my own mother, who I hadn't seen since I was seven.

Yeah, one dank day in February Mom told me to pack up a few things because we were going on a "big adventure." I filled a small suitcase with some clothes and then Mom told me to take my favorite books, toys and stuffed animals, too; we put those in a Macy's shopping bag. We took a cab up to Penn Station — I knew something was up because we *never* took cabs — and rode out to Hempstead where she deposited me with my father's older sister, who smelled like beer and cigarettes and showed me to a bedroom off the finished basement that had one high window and smelled like heating oil. Mom kissed me a thousand times and then left.

I haven't seen her since. The first year there were postcards from Ibiza and Goa telling me how much she missed me. I guess she stopped missing me — or maybe she was killed, that happens to loose girls in foreign countries, they get swallowed up, never to be heard from again. I hope she isn't dead. If she is alive, sometimes I wonder if she ever thinks of me. Ever wonders what happened to me, how I'm doing.

The bottom line here is that I don't know *how* to be a parent — Aunt Connie and the other beaten-down relatives who took turns raising me were hardly an example — and the idea of on-the-job training scared the hell out of me. I'd seen too many clients who'd been deeply scarred by even well-meaning moms to want to put my ambivalence to the test. Finally there was that little trauma from my past, the thing I hadn't told Zack or Abba or George or pretty much anyone else, the great sadness, guilt, regret that I'd pushed to the far side of my consciousness for twenty-seven years, where it remained, out of sight, out of mind, out of heart. Yeah right.

I knew it was pretty damn ironic that I preach making peace with our psychological traumas and moving forward with them, rather than denying them or pretending we can resolve them completely, and here I was carrying around this emotional lockbox. The difference was I *knew* and acknowledged that I hadn't faced down the demons. I planned to, in my own time and on my own terms. Really, I did.

But Josie had upended the equation, goddamn it, she'd touched me in some way I just couldn't ignore. She'd had a childhood of neglect and abuse — and had the bum leg to prove it — yet there was no self-pity there, just a feisty kid trying to make some sense of the world and find her place in it. I wanted to help her in any way I could.

I drove across the Hudson and into Troy. It's one of those cool old upstate cities, once-prosperous, now struggling, but filled with amazing character — brownstone townhouses, granite commercial buildings, brick factories, leafy squares, odd old stables and Masonic halls, tight-knit little 'hoods (including a really little Little Italy) — all overlain with a patina of history, loss, quietude, moxie, and a hint of menace. Troy looked like it was holding its own, maybe because Rensselaer Polytech, one of the country's best engineering colleges, sits on a hill above downtown and pumps enough dough into the city to keep despair at bay.

Josie's foster parents, Roberta and Doug Malden, lived just outside downtown. Their street was lined with small nondescript houses fronted by small yards, some well-kept, others in various states of decrepitude. I found neighborhoods like this depressing, you could almost smell the struggle and, unlike the downtown, there was no romance, no faded glory, just a sense of weary resignation, of a place where nobody was dreaming the American Dream anymore.

I found the Maldens' house. It was tidy in a blank sort of way, with polyester curtains in the front windows and two flowerboxes filled with straggly red and white impatiens. I knocked on the front door. A woman who looked about my age answered. She was plain, bespectacled, and slightly overweight, wearing a white blouse and navy slacks.

"Hi, Roberta, I'm Janet."

"Yes, I know that," she said flatly. What a charmer.

"Is Josie around?"

"She's inside."

"We're going out to lunch."

"Don't keep her long. She has chores and homework."

I looked over Roberta's shoulder and saw Josie sitting on a plaid couch with her hands in her lap. I smiled at her and she smiled back — a hint of mischief in her eyes. God, that was good to see.

I wanted to say something snarky and sarcastic to the gatekeeper, but held my tongue.

Roberta just stood there and so finally I said, "Well, are you going to let me in, or let Josie out?"

She pursed her lips and turned, I followed her into the house; it was neat and orderly and smelled like air freshener, there was a crucifix on the wall above the TV. Josie stood up.

"Hey, kiddo," I said.

"Hi, Janet."

She looked pretty good, her face had filled out a little, her clothes were clean, her eyes were bright. I was grateful to the Maldens. What they couldn't contain was Josie's restless curiosity and will — it radiated off her in waves.

"Hungry?"

"Famished."

"You had a good breakfast," Roberta said.

"She's a growing girl," I said, taking Josie's hand and leading her out.

We found an almost-charming faux-bistro

called Chez Fred downtown, I gave Josie the cellphone I'd bought for her, and she ordered practically everything on the menu. Watching her devour her salad filled me with some kind of bone-deep happiness I couldn't quite figure out; I could have sat there forever. Between bites, she filled me in on school — not very challenging; and the Maldens — ditto.

"They make me sad," she said. "They're so afraid."

"There's a lot of that going around."

"They only let me watch certain TV shows, they don't trust books and they put all sorts of filters on my computer."

"It's only for another three years, then you can go away to college."

She nodded, then looked down.

"You didn't get the shoes to even out your leg," I said.

"Their insurance won't cover it."

"*I'll* cover it, Josie. I want you to call an orthopedist on Monday. I mean it."

"Thank you. Now tell me *everything* that's happening down in Sawyerville."

I filled her in on the gang and also on Natasha Wolfson. She leaned across the table, hanging on every word, eyes sparkling, her face alive — she looked like a different girl from the one who'd sat on the couch with her hands in her lap.

When I was done, she was silent for a minute, then said, "How sure are you that it was murder?"

"I can't be 100 percent sure, of course, but my gut — and the fact that Natasha was mixed up with so many dubious characters — has me leaning strongly in that direction."

"You have to find out who the politician is, of course. And where Pavel was the night she died." I could see her mind racing over all the possibilities. "Let's assume it was murder. It's hard to imagine either Collier or Octavia would be up on a mountain."

"Then again, when passion is high people find strength they didn't know they had." She attacked her roast chicken, took a big bite, and said, "Take me back with you."

I froze and then managed: "Today?"

"Yeah. Let's just walk out of here, head to your car, and drive straight down to Sawyerville."

Whoa. I felt sweat break out under my arms and along my hairline. The idea was thrilling. Just get in the car, floor it, and bring Josie home. I looked her in the eyes — she was throwing me a serious challenge.

I had an impulsive streak a mile wide and over the years it had gotten me into a lot of trouble. It took time and therapy, but I'd learned how to rein it in. I took a deep breath. I didn't know the intricacies or legalities of the foster-parent system. Would it be breaking the law to just spirit this kid away with me? Was it fair to the Maldens? They were well-meaning in their own constricted way. Plus, did I really want Josie back 24/7? Yeah, she was no trouble and helpful as hell and good company, but I didn't want to be her goddamn mom, did I?

"Wouldn't that be breaking the law?"

"No. Foster children have the right to find their own living situation. I would inform my case worker and petition family court. They would pay you a visit. Done deal."

So she'd looked into the legalities. I just sat there for a moment taking it all in before asking, "How about dessert?"

Josie laughed, hard and deep, and I had to join her. Sitting in the slanted afternoon sun in Chez Fred we shared a laugh that lifted my spirits right out through the roof and tossed them up into the cloud-splattered Hudson Valley sky.

"Janet, you *need* me. You don't really care about that shop and you know it. *Things* don't really interest and excite you, *people* do. And, yes, I'll take the carrot cake. And a bowl of vanilla ice cream with hot fudge sauce."

"Anything else?"

She leaned across the table, put her hand on mine and said, "Sawyerville."

I felt a huge wave starting somewhere deep inside me, something so strong it scared me.

"Josie, I have to take a quick walk around the block, I'll be right back."

I gulped air as I strode around the side of the building into an alley. Then the tears just exploded, came and came and came, pouring out of me and over me, swamping me, drowning me, I loved that kid, goddamn it, and she loved *me* and I loved my baby, my baby . . .

Oh fuck, oh fuck . . .

I started walking again, the tears drying almost as quickly as they'd come. I was not going down *that* alley, no-way no-how, not now. I was a big girl, I'd gotten this far, built a decent life for myself, and I was going to protect it. That's just the way it had to be. I had a lot to give, but I couldn't give it all. Then what would be left for me?

I took my time getting around the block, used it to compose myself. When I arrived back at the table, Josie's desserts were untouched. I sat down and looked at her.

"Not today," I said. "But we'll keep the dialogue open. Now that you've got a cell it will be a lot simpler."

Josie looked down, her jaw tightened, then she looked up at me and nodded, "Fair enough."

She was making it easy for me. I should have known she would.

"Hey, your ice cream is melting."

She picked up the dish and began to slowly swirl the hot fudge into the vanilla ice cream.

I watched her for a minute, then turned and signaled for the check.

TWENTY

Even though it's got a pretty serious case of the cutes — you know, all historic and gift shoppy — there's no denying that Cold Spring is a charming village with a fantastic location. It sits on a little peninsula that juts out into the river, smack in the middle of the Hudson Highlands, mountains that rise straight up from the river on both banks and are famous as the home of West Point. The Highlands are gorgeous, mostly protected land; they kind of squeeze the Hudson, creating its narrowest point, so narrow that during the Revolutionary War the good guys strung heavy iron chain across it to stop the British ships from getting upriver.

These days Cold Spring is a hopping little burg that lives on tourists who train up from the city for a day of shopping and strolling. Natasha's memorial was being held at a place called Glynwood, a farm a few miles out of town.

I turned down Glynwood's drive — the place was so bucolic it made me want to kill myself. Apparently it was originally some rich guy's toy farm and now it was a center working to help save farms all up and down the valley. Tip of the hat there, huh? I parked and walked to the large old barn where the memorial was being held. The people milling around were pretty much divided into two groups: youngish hipster/musician types, no doubt Natasha's buddies; older sophisticate/media types who were her parents' crowd. I semi-recognized a few semi-famous faces.

Then I spotted Howard and Sally Wolfson outside the barn greeting people. I'd Googled them and knew he was late-fifties, she ten years younger, in person they both looked groomed and botoxed and nip-tucked, not quite real in that way celebrities do in person. He was a handsome guy, had a fatherly schtick going: gray-hair, friendly, going a little soft around the middle. She was working a Martha Stewarty vibe, with highlighted hair in a soft cut, expert make-up, pretty in a nonthreatening way, wearing tasteful black separates. They both looked like they were in mild shock, their faces taut with grief — or some reasonable facsimile.

I knew from my Googling that the Wolfsons had another daughter and there she was, Natasha's younger sister, Julia, standing a few feet away from her parents. She was tall, blonde, pretty in an upper-middle-class way, but too thin, jumpy, sweaty around the edges, her eyes scanning the arrivals, wearing a short black dress and too-high heels. Her phone rang, she answered it, said a few words, and hung up.

I made my way toward the parents.

"Hi, I'm Janet Petrocelli, a friend of your daughter."

"Thank you for coming," Howard said.

"It means a lot to us," Sally said.

"Natasha was a lovely young woman. I wanted to mention that I owed her some money, and I have some jewelry that belonged to her."

Sally's eyebrows went up. And the sister, ears twitching, stepped closer.

"I'm Julia Wolfson, Natasha's kid sister. She had such cool jewelry. Can I take a look at it?"

Sally Wolfson shot her a frigid glance and said *sotto voce,* "This is *not* the time, Julia." Then she turned to me, "Can you come to the house after the service? We're having just a few people up," she said, cunningly making me feel like one of the chosen.

Inside the barn Natasha's music was playing, her soulful voice enriched by glorious acoustics. There were boards set up with pictures of her life: the family pictures had a posed, slightly forced feel, with Sally and Howard front and center; in shots from Natasha's early career she was simply stunning, that amazing raven hair, dark eyes, white skin; there were stills from her concerts and TV appearances, rave reviews and clippings, shots of her with people like David Byrne, Beck, Charlotte Gainsbourg, Michael Stipe.

I took a seat. The service started with a woman who'd been a childhood friend, who told stories of Natasha's little girl tea parties, where the guests included not only dolls but hamsters, guinea pigs, and ghosts, and where the tea was spiced with maple syrup masquerading as rum. I was clocking the Wolfsons in the front row — they were arm-in-arm but at one point Sally leaned against Howard's shoulder and he leaned away; Julia could barely sit still, she'd slap on a listening face for a few moments, then sneak a glance at her phone, run her fingers through her hair, her crossed leg bouncing.

This kid in his mid-twenties, thin, wearing skinny jeans, sneakers, striped top, hip hat, took the platform.

"Hey, people, I'm Joey Frank, and Natasha was just about the first person I met when I moved to New York from Camden and I didn't know one single person and I had forty bucks in my pocket. I spent my first week sleeping in Tompkins Square Park, that was fun, all I knew was that I wanted to make music. Natasha heard me playing and man she took my hand and showed me the city, we walked all the hell over the place — like museums, I'd never been in a museum in my life — and at night she took me to the clubs to hear music and introduced me to everyone she knew in the business. She was my downtown angel, my beautiful black-haired angel." He looked down, bit his lip, the place was pin-drop quiet. "She showed me the city, she showed me the business, she showed me life and art, and she taught me that it was okay to be soft and open and to let people in. Hey, I live in LA now and you know my songs have been done by some pretty big people, I'm doing good, real good, and it wouldn't have happened, it just wouldn't have, without my black-haired angel." He looked up. "Goodbye, Natasha."

The service ended with a group of musicians singing *Love by Any Other Name.* I remembered that morning in Phoenicia, just a week ago, her voice, the way she moved around the room, swept up in the music, her kind soulful eyes.

I was going to find out the truth about her death — and if she was murdered, there was no way the killer was going to walk.

Then it was over. Her friends were reluctant to leave and you could feel the reason why: they wanted to hold onto her, to the sweet sad moment of shared loss.

I got in my car and followed a small caravan that was heading to the Wolfson's house. We drove several miles up into the Highlands before coming to a bold mid-century house that jutted out from the hillside and seemed to hang over the mountain and the Hudson below.

The cars were mostly fancy, the people getting out mostly older, with the sparkly glaze of success, chatting, smiling, already on to the next thing — for most this was clearly a duty call. Julia was in a corner of the drive, facing away from everyone, hunched over, talking on her cell.

The inside of the house was pretty stunning, all swoops and window walls, teak, low couches, abstract rugs, striking accents, a view out over the river that made my breath catch. The sophisticated décor belied the approachable, Middle-American image that the Wolfsons presented as their public personas.

Cater waiters in uniforms were offering up trays of hors d'oeuvres and glasses of wine. Sally and Howard sat front and center on a vast armless couch, receiving condolences. Sally motioned over one of the servers and took a glass of wine. She leaned into her husband and whispered something.

I felt like I was on the wrong planet, underdressed, I didn't know a soul, I hovered in a corner, grabbed a crab cake off a passing tray and pretended to be really involved in eating it.

"Terribly sad, isn't it?" a woman said, coming up to me. She was full-bodied, older, gray-hair pulled back into a chignon, chic gray knit dress, fabulous geometric jewelry.

I nodded.

She looked me over, "Do you work for Howard and Sally?"

I made a decision not to be offended — I was here to gather info — maybe she had some. "I'm a friend of Natasha's."

"Oh. Are you in the music business?"

"I'm not. Did you know Natasha well?"

"No, I'm a more recent friend of Howard and Sally. We're on several local boards together."

"They must be devastated."

She paused and took a sip of her wine. This gal wanted to get down a little, I could smell it, that's probably why she beelined for scruffy out-of-place me, it's always easier to open up to the serving classes — you never have to see them again.

"I hope it brings them together," she said, giving me a meaningful glance.

Bingo. "I'd heard there were some problems in the marriage."

"He's at that age."

"The now-or-never stage?"

She gave me an almost imperceptible nod. "When my husband went through it I kicked him right out the door."

"But their careers are co-dependent, so Sally can't do that, can she?"

"You certainly understand the situation. I suppose Natasha told you all about them."

"It wasn't easy having them for parents."

"I expect it wasn't. Sometimes at a board meeting Sally will just start talking about herself, apropos of absolutely nothing. It's a bit . . . showy. Strange even. One wonders." She spied someone across the room and turned and walked away without a word, probably feeling a bit of gossip's remorse.

And then Julia Wolfson was next to me. Her eyes were bright and shining, kid was definitely on some kind of upper, I guessed coke.

"Natasha died without a will, everything goes to Mom and Dad. Like they need it. Can I take a look at that jewelry? I'm an actress," she laughed, awkward, "but between jobs I buy and sell stuff, in the city, I work with shops and stuff, downtown, Lower East Side, East Village, Natasha had a great eye, she had a great everything, right."

"It's between you and your folks."

"There's nothing between me and my folks."

"Was there with Natasha?"

"Natasha was the star. Even when she fucked up, she was the star. I fucked up and I'm still the understudy." She laughed, bitter. "Do you have a card?"

Boy, she sure wasn't mourning her sister much. "My store is in Sawyerville, it's called Janet's Planet."

Howard Wolfson appeared. He looked exhausted and sad but still working the room. A-types never cease to amaze me. "Julia, your cousin is looking for you." Julia walked away. He smiled at me, "So you owed Natasha some money."

"Yes, I bought some jewelry from her and she died before I could pay her."

"How much money are we talking about?"

"Three thousand dollars. Unless you want what's left of the jewelry back."

He turned away and said goodbye to a departing guest. When he turned back he seemed distracted, as if I was a minor nuisance.

"Why don't you send us a check."

"I'll do that."

"Thank you for coming," he said, dismissing me.

As I left I saw Sally check her watch.

Twenty-One

I hit Chow the next morning and was sitting at the counter waiting (and waiting) for Pearl to get me a cup of coffee when Abba came out from the kitchen with a map in her hand.

"So Kelly's Farm does exist," she said, opening the map — which was topographic and detailed, showing every house — laying it out on the counter, and pointing to a tiny dot in what looked an uninhabited corner of Delaware County, "It's way the hell up here."

"That's pretty isolated."

"And it's going to stay that way, that valley is completely surrounded by state land."

"Did you find out anything else?"

"Nothing from a customer's mouth, but there are lots of rumors that it's a house of pleasure . . . and pain."

"Something tells me I'm going to have to pay a little visit."

"Be careful. You could be mixing with some seriously dangerous characters, Janet."
"I'll keep my wits — and my kickboxing — about me."
"So, how did it go with Josie?"
I filled her in on the visit.
"Why do I get the feeling you're holding out on me?" she asked.
"Because you have a good imagination."
"It doesn't take imagination, it takes being your friend."
Thankfully my coffee arrived. I added way too much milk and sugar.
"Listen, if there's ever anything you want to talk about, you know where to find me," Abba said.
"Yeah-yeah," I mumbled.
Thankfully George strutted in wearing his jodhpurs, a riding helmet, and carrying a crop.
"Good morning, ladies!" he slapped his thigh with his crop and burst into song lyrics about wild horses that couldn't drag him away.
"Could a fennel-cheddar omelet?" Abba asked.
"No, but I'll have one. With a short stack, bacon, grits, and hash browns. I need my strength today, I'm having my first riding lesson with a *real* horse."

"Hey, that's fantastic," I said.

George puffed up like a little potentate.

"Out at the horse show?" Abba asked.

George gave his head a little shake, almost like a pony tossing its mane.

"Where then?" I asked.

"Janet, you always make me feel like I'm being interrogated by the CIA."

"Blame the questioner."

"You're damn right I blame the questioner. I have met the love of my life and instead of embracing my bliss, you try to diminish it with irrelevant questions."

"I just asked where you were going to take your riding lesson?"

"At a horse farm out in Blue Mountain. *Okay!* Are you happy now?"

"Oh, which one?" Abba asked.

"Shouldn't you be working on my omelet?"

Abba shot me a bemused look as she got up and headed into the kitchen, saying over her shoulder, "Blue Mountain Stables has an incredible reputation . . . as a breeder of miniature horses."

George ignored this, jutted out his chest and chin and sat down on the stool next to mine. "Pearl, may I have a *café con leche, por favor?*" She looked at him like he was speaking Martian. "A cup of coffee, for

Christ's sake!"

"I didn't think adults could ride miniature horses," I said.

"I said it was my first riding lesson *with* a real horse, not *on* a real horse. It's a slow process of acclimatization."

"I'm sure it'll be great."

"Don't patronize me."

"How's the Van Wyck campaign going?"

"I think he's going to win, but he wants to win big to set himself up for his next move. I've only met him a couple of times but he seems pretty real, for a politician. And on the issues, he's amazing. His ambition is a little scary, but ambition usually is." His coffee arrived and he took a sip. "How's your investigation going?"

"It's expanding." I filled him in on Natasha's memorial and Kelly's Farm.

"Let me know if you need my help with anything. Kelly's Farm sounds intriguing. Personally I could never get into S&M — too many accoutrements."

I eyeballed his riding gear.

He gave me a *mea culpa* smile and said, "It's a good thing you're cute."

I walked from Chow through the village and then down the road leading to the Sawyersville lighthouse. It was fun walking around town and the road down to the lighthouse wound above the Esopus Creek so it was especially cool. The lighthouse sits at the end of a spit of land that sticks out into the Hudson almost half a mile. The Hudson is tidal even this far up, and at high tide things can get sloppy. But I wasn't headed to the lighthouse today — I was looking to pay Mad John a visit.

I walked a little ways down the lighthouse path and then veered north, heading into the riverside snarl, ducking brush and branches, until I came to a tattered rubber-ducky shower curtain strung between two trees: Mad John's front door.

"Knock-knock."

"I'm up here, Jan-Jan."

I looked up into the trees and there was Mad John sitting on a branch with a raccoon in his lap. The critter was sprawled on its back and Mad John was scratching its tummy.

"Edgar loves this," he said.

"I need your help."

He righted Edgar and they clambered down the tree together, looking more like distant cousins than different species. He pulled back the shower curtain and ushered me into his digs, a little encampment furnished with rusty lawn chairs, ratty rugs, and a primitive ever-changing altar that currently featured the Indian goddess Kali, a bobble-head Ringo Starr, and a plastic turd.

"What's up, chowdahead?" he asked.

I opened the map and spread it out on a rug. "Do you know where this is?" I asked, pointing to the distant valley.

Mad John pulled on his beard and pondered for a moment. Then he started his ecstatic jumping up and down thing, "Catskills-Catskills-Catskills!"

Edgar, busying himself with an overripe banana — Mad John was a world-class dumpster diver — looked over in bemusement.

"See this farmhouse, I want to do a little reconnoiter, but on the down low. Do you think you could get me there through the woods?"

He froze and eyeballed me intently, then went right back to jumping, "Bushwhack–bushwhack-bushwhack!"

"I take it that's a yes?"

He jumped up and clicked his heels (well, thumped his barefeet), "Hot cha-cha-cha!"

"Does tomorrow work for you?" I asked.

"I'll have to check with my secretary."

"I'll pick you up in the afternoon, I think we should get there at dusk."

As I walked away I heard, "Hey, Edgar, wanna go fishing?"

Twenty-Two

I headed back to town and opened the store — it's always good to put in an appearance at your own establishment. I put on some tango and paid attention to Bub and Sputnik while Lois sat on her favorite armchair giving us the evil eye. Looking at her I couldn't help thinking: she'd make an adorable throw rug. The phone rang.

"Janet's Planet."

"Hi, it's Josie. I found out a few interesting things about Collier Denton. In 1979, the actor Ian Stock who was the star of the soap opera *The Well Runs Deep* died in a suspicious fire at his house in Sneden's Landing. Two weeks later his part was recast with Collier Denton."

I flashed on the scar on Denton's left forearm.

"And no determination was ever made as to the cause of the fire?"

"Stock was a smoker and forensics was

able to determine that the fire originated in his bedroom, but his body was so badly incinerated that medical examiners were unable to establish a definitive cause of death. No charges were ever filed."

"Incredible. What's the other info?"

"In 1998, Collier Denton's 'roommate' died in a mysterious fall at his house in Stone Ridge. There was a police investigation and a manslaughter charge was under consideration, but never filed."

"Any other details?"

"The deceased's name was Tony Ramirez. He was twenty-two years old, Dominican, unemployed, he and Denton had met in Miami Beach the year before. He fell down the house's back stairs, which are very steep, and died of a cerebral hemorrhage. Denton didn't call the police for two hours."

"He was probably waiting to sober up."

"That's just what I was thinking."

"Good work, Josie."

"Talk to you later."

So Collier Denton was not only a sleazebag, he might be capable of manslaughter or even murder. I went back to my workroom and started to wax a table, physical work tends to clear my head, which needed it, cluttered as it was with information, innuendo, and suspicion. The bell rang out in the shop and since my wheels were spinning in place I welcomed the interruption.

I went out to find Julia Wolfson looking around. She was wearing a tight black skirt, black ankle boots, a shimmery purple blouse, too much make-up — she was way overdressed for Sawyerville. She was a little less jittery, but not much, gave me a too-big smile and said, "You've got some really cool stuff. And chill town, so authentic. Oh look!" she said, her attention ricocheting to Bub. She went over and scratched his chest, he smiled in delight.

"That's Bub."

"I've never had a bird." Sputnik approached her. "We had a dog when we were little but it shit in the kitchen and Sally sent it back. Can I smoke in here?"

I shrugged.

She took out some hip English brand and lit up. "I don't smoke. Boy, yesterday was a freak show. My parents just push every button I have, all at once."

"They're dynamic people."

"They're self-obsessed freaks. Every time I see them on television I get nauseous. I can't believe anyone buys their bullshit. That was the first time I'd been in their house in two years." She walked around the store, eyeing stuff, picking up stuff, putting it back, ADHD in overdrive.

"They're busy people."

"Not as busy as they used to be, ha-ha. Their books don't sell like they used to and the TV gigs are drying up; they're kind of bugging out about it, especially Sally, plus you know she's getting old and I think Dad is fucking someone on the side."

"Is it serious?"

"Who knows. I wish Sally would get some on the side herself, but she's still bug-eyed for the old man. It's hitting her hard, she's even more tense than she used to be. Suddenly she wants to be my 'friend.' I mean how sick is that, she was barely my mother, and now she wants to be my *friend.*" She gave a bitter snort of a laugh.

"Did she and Natasha get along?"

"Not really. Sally put on a good game when people were around, but it was all playacting. Hey look, I've been in rehab, I know the drill: she had a traumatic childhood, was never really parented herself, she did her best blah-blah-blah."

"What was traumatic about her childhood?"

She turned away from me, examined a chrome lamp, "I don't know the details." She took a deep pull on her cigarette. "I mean at this point who really gives a fuck, right?"

"Were you and Natasha close when you were little?"

"I never really knew her too well, isn't that weird, I mean I'm four years younger, Sally pitted us against each other, we were sent away to different boarding schools. I kind of idolized Natasha, I mean she was pretty cool, she used to send me letters from school, funny shit, she called me Sis Kid, and at holidays we would have some fun together." She plopped down on a sofa and ran her hand over the fabric; I got the feeling she was holding out on me.

"What about your dad?"

"What about him?" she said, quick, defensive.

"Did he and Natasha get along?"

She was silent for a moment and then said quietly, "You'd have to ask him. . . . Were you close with her?"

"I only met her once, the day before she died, but she made an impression, I liked her a lot."

"Oh, I loved her and all that, but, you know . . ." She leapt up, opened the shop door and flicked her cigarette out into the street. "These boots are Versace, I got them at Housing Works, forty bucks."

"When did you last see her?"

"A few months ago." She walked over to a display case, "Is this her jewelry?"

"Yes."

"It's gorgeous, it reminds me of her. Can I have it?"

"I told your folks I'd send them a check for it."

"Fuck them. They shit money." She looked at me, clenching her jaw. "Send them less. Their checks go right to an accountant. They'll never notice. What do you think — they're going to come after you?"

"I think it's between you and them."

"Well, I'd call them up except I don't have their cell numbers."

"What about their land line?"

"They don't have a land line. I mean they do, but it's to their office and their manager's secretary answers it." She sat down again, lit a fresh cigarette, and looked like she was about to cry. "I haven't had an acting gig in awhile, I'm twenty-five fucking years old and living on ether, I could sell this jewelry in the city for decent cash." She eyeballed me — her need acute, her sadness infinite.

"Go ahead, take the jewelry."

She went over to the case and opened it, stuck the cigarette between her lips and shoveled the jewelry into her bag. "Oh man, you don't know how much I appreciate this." She came over and gave me a quick hug, I could feel her bones, then she just about ran out of the store, cigarette dangling from her mouth, reaching into her bag, pulling out her cell.

Sputnik watched her go, then turned and gave me a questioning look.

Twenty-Three

Mad John and I drove deep into the Catskills. It's strange and beautiful up there, towns so small and empty that they almost feel abandoned, a smattering of farms, prefabs with plastic over the windows, gorgeous mountains and streams — there's something scary about all the openness, beauty tinged with terror, *Night of the Living Dead* in *Brigadoon.*

Mad John had brought a machete and was in high spirits.

"Where we going?" he asked.

"To a whorehouse."

"Do they take checks?"

We laughed. "No handling the merchandise, young man. I want to scope the place out, get a sense of how it operates, take some pictures. What I'd really like is to get inside and find the little black book."

The afternoon was waning, the light growing denser, the air pouring in the car windows drier than down in the valley, with each mile it got more remote and rural; out here there was no one to hear you scream. Men drove into this isolation to get tied up, beaten, humiliated, away from the eyes of their wives and girlfriends, of the world, of themselves. It would be a whole lot healthier if they'd just get their wives to do the beating — I'd worked with clients who'd revealed their secret lusts to their spouses, who were usually happy to oblige. But I guess healthy wasn't what these men craved.

We reached the mouth of the mountain valley; Kelly's Farm was about three miles up a narrow road. I found an old dirt track and drove down it far enough to be out of sight. We got out of the car. The woods looked awfully dense. I'd brought two flashlights and a pair of binoculars along.

"Are you sure you're going to be able to get us in *and* out?"

Mad John just gave me a huge grin and took a whack at the underbrush, which disappeared like magic. I had complete faith in his outdoor skills, I just wished I had the same faith in my own sleuthing skills. But Natasha had worked at this place and I needed to know who her clients were and I sure as hell wasn't going to get the information by asking.

We set off through the woods, gallant little Mad John in the lead, machete swinging, carrying on a running conversation with the local avian population. I find woods a huge bore, but the terrain and my own mounting anxiety kept me alert and after awhile I went into a sort of fugue state, one foot in front of the other.

Then Mad John stopped and *hissssss*-ed.

Up ahead the woods ended and an old farmstead began — there were fields, stone walls, a couple of cows and goats grazing, a hen house, several barns and outbuildings, and a large old farmhouse. About half a dozen cars were parked out front. The place was in good repair but hardly had that Currier-and-Ives look you get when rich city folk tart-up an old farm, it just looked like an old farm that was somehow hanging in there.

"Let's just chill here and see what happens," I said, feeling pretty unchill. It looked like we had about another half-hour of daylight, which was perfect timing, I could plan my steps and then take them under cover of dark.

The house was rambling, with a rear wing that led to a screened breezeway that connected it to a barn. I raised my binocs: lights were on in the front of the house and the rooms looked perfectly ordinary. I'm not sure what I was expecting — red velvet walls and fringed lampshades maybe — but it looked more like Mayberry with corduroy couches, reproduction rockers, a massive TV. Behind the living room, there was a cozy claustrophobic kitchen with yellow walls, floral curtains, decorative trivets on the wall.

I moved my sights farther back in the house — the windows were blackened, either with paint or fabric. I came to the breezeway and saw a tall, buxom not-young woman holding a leash at the end of which crawled a hairy, paunchy, middle-aged man wearing a diaper and a baby bonnet with a pacifier in his mouth. Fun. She led him into the barn.

There were no lights on upstairs so I couldn't tell what the rooms looked like. What I wanted to find was the office. Oh yeah, and I should probably photograph the license plates on the cars.

Night had fallen, a dark night with just a sliver moon — it was time to make my move.

"Mad John, can you wait for me here? I shouldn't be more than half an hour."

I set out across the lawn in a running crouch, avoiding the pools of light casting out from the windows, my heart thumping in my chest, my breathing shallow. I headed to the driveway, took out my cell and photographed the license plates.

I headed around the other side of the house and moved in close — sure enough, through a window I saw an office: desk, computer, printer, fax, all neat, orderly, professional. There was a large datebook open on the desk, with several other ledgers nearby. The door leading from the office into the rest of the house was closed. I stepped closer to the window and was about to reach up to try and push it open when I felt a hand on my shoulder.

"Hi, Fran."

I practically jumped out of my skin. I spun around to see a lumpy old woman in a loose housedress and slippers, her eyes vacant, her mouth open. It took me only a second to realize that this gal had Alzheimer's and was on a twilight ramble.

"I'm sorry, I'm not Fran."

She bit her lower lip and tears started to slip from her eyes. Man, that disease is a heartbreaker. But I had to get us away from the house.

"Listen, I'm kind of here on business," I whispered, "but do you want to take a little walk or something?"

She nodded. I took her hand and led her toward the edge of the field, where Mad John waited.

"*Psst!* Can you take this lady?"

Mad John appeared and gave her a huge grin. She smiled back. He took her hand and held it to his cheek, she purred.

I headed back toward the house. Then the front door opened, a woman's silhouette appeared in the doorway and the beam of a flashlight swept over the lawn. "Ma, you out there?" Then the beam landed right on me. "Who're you?"

"Hi, I'm Janet," I said, trying to sound nonchalant.

"What can I do for you, Janet?" The lady sounded pretty damn nonchalant herself. I walked toward her and she lowered the flashlight. She was about my age, average looking, shapely with some middle-aged spread, the kind of person you wouldn't look twice at in the supermarket.

"I was just, um, walking around."

"You were, huh? Did you happen to see my mom?"

"Yes, she's with my friend over there, I think they hit it off."

She aimed her beam across the field — Mad John and her mom were communing with one of the goats. "That's nice. Now you want to come in and tell me what the hell you're doing on my farm?"

"Ah, sure."

She led me into the living room, a basketball game was on the television. She muted it. "I'm Kelly. Have a seat." I sat on a sofa, she sat across from me on a lounger. There were bowls of Chex mix on the coffee table in front of me and on the table next to her. "Help yourself to some Chex mix."

"I'm good, thanks."

"I like your friend, anyone who can calm Mom down is okay in my book."

"He's a great guy."

"So, what's up?"

"I'm a friend of Natasha Wolfson."

She took this in and looked at me, I held her gaze. I sensed she was trying to dope out how much I knew. She nodded to herself, seeming to decide there was no point in playing pretend. "I was sorry to lose her, she was a nice girl."

"I think she may have been murdered."

"Do you?"

"Yes. I want to rule out any of her clients, johns, whatever-you-call-them."

"I call them customers."

"Can you let me know who Natasha's regulars were?"

"Are you kidding? Part of what I'm selling

here is discretion."

"So you'd protect a murderer?"

"I'd protect my business." She got up and crossed the room, stood over me. "Can I see your cellphone?" Her tone was mild, but her eyes weren't.

"What cellphone?"

"The one I'm assuming you photographed the license plates with." I handed it to her, she quickly deleted the shots and handed it back.

"So you won't give me the information I need?"

"Here's all the information you need: This farm is my life and my livelihood."

I decided to change tack, took a handful of Chex mix. "This is delicious."

"I add paprika." She walked back to her lounger.

"So how long you been running Kelly's Farm?"

She was on to me and smiled, "If it weren't for your little friend amusing Mom, you'd be outta here." She scooped a handful of Chex mix from the bowl next to her and checked out the basketball score on the television. "This farm's been in my family for over two hundred years."

"That's a long time."

"Too long. The only crop that thrives in

this lousy soil is poverty."

"So you added a sideline?"

"You might say that." In spite of herself she was warming up — if you come at them right, *everybody* likes to talk. "I started it as a bed and breakfast after my husband disappeared. City folks were *paying* me to shovel manure." She laughed and scooped another handful of the mix. "Then one day I discovered this guest out in the barn, well . . . let's just say he was sweet on one of my cows. He was so ashamed he paid me a tidy sum to forget what I saw. One thing led to another."

I felt my blood pressure rise. "Do you still pimp out your animals?"

"What's it to you?"

"A deal breaker."

"Well, don't bust a gasket. Anyone who grew up on a farm knows these things happen, but my animals are strictly off limits. But otherwise pretty much anything goes as long as nobody gets hurt — unless they want to." A muffled scream echoed from somewhere in the far reaches of the farm. She sat back and crossed her arms with pride. "It's worked out — I put my three kids through college, take care of my mom, and I'm socking away enough to buy me a nice place down in the Keys."

"That's all great, but if Natasha was murdered, I still want to nail whoever did it."

"You mess with my meal ticket, I will take you out."

"Is that a threat?"

"It's a promise."

"I can do this without bringing you into it," I said.

"Once oil spills it tends to spread."

"What if I gave you my word?"

"I'd give it back."

"I could go to the cops."

"Now who's the one making threats? And the cops aren't going to touch me, not after two hundred years, and not with the goods I got."

There was a knock from the direction of the kitchen. "Stay put," she said with a tight smile, an iron fist in an oven mitt. She got up, went into the kitchen and I heard, "Gimme ten minutes." She walked back into the living room. "Party's over. I assume we understand each other."

"I'm not sure you understand how I feel about murder."

"Well, as long as you understand how *I* feel about protecting my farm, we'll get along just fine. Now where's your car?"

"Down at the head of the valley."

"I'll drive you down."
"We can walk."
"Don't push your luck."
As soon as Mad John and I were in my car and headed back to Sawyerville, he started rattling off numbers. I gave him a questioning look.
"The license plates," he said.
"You're brilliant."
"I know."
Then he started bouncing up and down on his seat.

Twenty-Four

I called Chevrona Williams the next morning and asked her if she could run the plates. She said she would and that she'd bring me the results in person in a couple of hours. I hung up, took a nice long bath filled with salts and lovely gels, washed my hair, put on some clean clothes and lipstick, I almost dabbed on a little perfume but thought that might seem cheap and obvious.

The phone rang.

"It's me," Josie said. "The Wolfsons have just signed a six-figure contract for a book about their daughter Natasha's life and suicide. It's called *Lost Child.*"

A chill raced up my spine. "Boy, they don't waste any time, do they? And they're labeling it a suicide."

"It probably makes it more saleable."

"Yeah. How are things going up there?"

"Better now that I have something to

obsess on."

"Oh God, you sound like me."

"No comment."

"Listen, thanks."

"Keep me posted."

I hung up and headed over to Chow. It was a very busy morning and Pearl was really struggling to keep up — of course she struggled to keep up when the place was empty. Abba waved me into the kitchen.

"Hey, you look pretty this morning," she said, juggling half a dozen orders.

"Dumb luck, I guess."

"You really are the world's worst fibber."

"Chevrona Williams is dropping over."

Abba just gave me one of her knowing smiles as she flipped an omelet with one hand and pancakes with the other.

"You've *got* to hire some help."

"I hear you. Wish I could find someone who could cook *and* wait tables. Someone like, say, Josie."

"But Josie lives in Troy."

Abba eyeballed me, "You and I have got to have a serious talk sometime in the very near future. I think you're fighting your own instincts."

Eager to change the subject, I filled her in on my trip to Kelly's Farm.

"I'd take what Kelly said very seriously,

you don't mess with those old backwoods gals. And I'm sure she wasn't bluffing when it came to both the local police and the power of her little black book."

"Yeah."

"Hey, I'm catering my first political fund-raiser, for Clark Van Wyck."

"Put humble pie on the menu."

Twenty-Five

When Chevrona walked into the store, I felt that little flutter I'd come to know and . . . feel ambivalent about. On the one hand, I didn't need any more romantic entanglements, I had a boyfriend, I'd never slept with a woman. On the other hand every time I got within ten feet of Chevrona, I felt this emotional pull. It was the way she looked down and rubbed the back of her neck, the way she narrowed her eyes and that dead-honest look in them, vulnerable and tough at the same time, and the sense that whatever she had she'd earned the hard way.

"Hi, Chevrona."

"Hi, Janet."

Channeling my feelings, Sputnik went shortcakes, jumping all over her.

"Did he drink too much of that amazing coffee of yours?" Chevrona asked.

"If I'd had a little more notice, I would

have gone out and bought gourmet. You want a cup?"

"I'll pass."

"So . . . how are you?"

"I'm good. You?"

"Good." Unless I was delusional, the force field between us was mutual. "Have a seat."

She sat and leaned forward, elbows on her knees, she was just so . . . masculine, in this unforced way men so rarely are, and feminine, too, in her sensitivity and empathy. "So, I ran the plates."

"And . . . ?"

"First, why don't you tell me where you saw them?"

"Do I have to?"

"Yes."

I gave her a quick overview of my investigation to date.

"Janet, you're wading into some treacherous waters here."

"I'm not going to let go of this."

"Did you know that Natasha Wolfson was hospitalized for acute drug-induced psychosis after a suicide attempt four years ago?"

I knew Natasha was troubled, but this information vaulted her into a whole new category. Was it possible she did throw herself off that ledge up on Platte Clove? "That's sad news. Why didn't you tell me?"

"I just found out yesterday."

"I guess this does increase the odds she committed suicide."

"That's what I thought. I've been back up to that mountaintop, I've walked it, been over it with a fine-tooth comb. There's just no evidence, no tire marks, footprints, fingerprints, nothing on the ground. When the body was recovered, the officers searched the pool for anything that may have been on Natasha's person, nothing was found."

"Was the entire length of the stream searched?"

"That's a long shot."

"What if Natasha grabbed at her killer as she fell and ripped off a piece of fabric, a watch, a piece of jewelry, and then it washed downstream?"

"Good point. I'll request that search be made. But I think you should leave it in our hands."

"The more hands the better."

She gave me one of her half-smiles. "On the record, I'm advising you to stop. Off the record, I admire the hell out of you."

She admired me.

"You want those plates?"

"Oh yeah, sure, of course."

"Now this will just show you who the cars

are *registered* to, which is not a guarantee that's who was on the premises last night."

"Gotcha."

She handed me a printout and one name leapt right out: Clark Van Wyck.

"Did you see this name? Clark Van Wyck is our very ambitious state senator," I said, feeling my adrenaline spike.

"With the very ambitious wife," Chevrona said. "I've heard she's determined to become the state's First Lady."

"If he was one of Natasha's regulars and he thought for some reason it might come out, you have a pretty strong motive for getting her out of the picture. And if the wife found out about his specialized tastes — well, that's math even I can handle."

"It's a long way from wanting someone out of the picture to murdering them."

"True. But doesn't it seem worth exploring? I'd at least like to find out if he was a client of Natasha's."

"That would be good to know. But the bottom line here is that if this was a murder, we need some *hard* evidence. It's tough to get a DA to run with a circumstantial argument. Without evidence, reasonable doubt is pretty plausible. When it comes to a murder conviction, juries are tough."

"Do you think it's hopeless?"

"It's not looking good so far. And Natasha's previous suicide attempt and hospitalization don't help. I'm not convinced this was murder, but if it was it may turn out that the best shot is to go under the radar, build a powerful circumstantial case, and use it to bluff out a confession."

We were quiet for a moment and then I said, "Well, now I know what I'm aiming for."

Twenty-Six

The next morning I hopped in my car for the quick forty-mile trip up to Albany.

Although I was focused on one thing — a certain state senator — I was always happy to visit Albany. From 1810 to 1850 it was one of the biggest cities in the country and its downtown has some cool vestiges of those boom days, like sylvan Washington Park and the brownstone neighborhoods that surround it. Being the state capital the town has a permanent safety net, so it's escaped that romantic melancholy place-that-time-forgot aura that hangs over so many struggling upstate towns. It also escaped the decimation of urban renewal, that 1960s fad that gutted scores of amazing old neighborhoods across the state and replaced them with soulless car-centric wastelands. Don't get me started.

I parked my car and crossed Empire State Plaza, which is always a thrill. The plaza is a *blast*, a stunning modernist expanse built by lovable hyperactive grandiose former governor Nelson Rockefeller — he who died with his pants off in the arms of his mistress. There's a vast reflecting pool in the center of the plaza, surrounded by four *identical* skyscrapers and an egg-shaped theater that balances on a narrow base, all anchored at one end by the airy arch-graced state museum and at the other by the state capitol, a massive Gothic-Romanesque pile designed by H. H. Richardson in 1899. All in all, Empire State Plaza is one of the great urban set pieces — fabulous and futuristic. Worth a detour.

I walked into the capitol and passed through security. This was my first time inside and I was kind of amazed at how grand and ornate the place was — lots of marble and tile and this *amazing* central staircase, carved red sandstone, with more landings and turns than an M. C. Escher. I walked past the senate chamber: plush, dignified, right out of a history book, it exudes gravity, wealth, the high ideals of laws and men, the days when New York State really was an empire.

Which makes it all the more ironic that today the capital is hack central, filled with sweaty sleazy cheesy politicos working every crooked angle to make themselves and their cronies not-even-rich. The folks I passed in the hallways were a dead giveaway — oblivious to their noble surroundings, they kept their heads down, their faces impassive, you could almost smell the guilt and corruption wafting around corners and through the air ducts. I peeked in a few offices — the gray faces "working" at their desktops looked like they were playing online poker, watching porn or buying new towels from overstock.com — or maybe all three at once.

I found Clark Van Wyck's office and walked in. The contrast was striking — freshly painted, bustling with wholesome staffers, the posters on the wall extolled the benefits of organic farming and wind power with the tagline "A *New* New York."

"Welcome," a friendly middle-aged receptionist said.

"Hi, I'm a constituent of Senator Van Wyck's and I was wondering if I could have a few minutes of his time?"

"May I ask what this is in reference to?" she asked.

"A farm in the district."

"Senator Van Wyck is *passionate* about saving our farms. May I have your name?"

"Janet Petrocelli."

"And where is the farm?"

"Delaware County."

"Hold on just a moment, please."

She got up, walked down a short hallway and was back in a jiff. "The senator would be delighted to see you."

Van Wyck's office was spotless, orderly, with a rolled-up yoga mat sitting ostentatiously on the couch, more *New* New York posters on the walls, pics of the senator and his wife with the Clintons, Cuomos, Obamas, Nelson Mandela, Deepak Chopra, George Clooney, Arianna Huffington. His desk was so awash in family pictures of him, his wife, and their three kids — on a Catskill peak, ziplining in the rain forest, serving turkey to the homeless — that I got he-doth-protest-too-much vibe. There was also an open Tiffany's catalogue on the desk.

The senator — boyish, lanky, pretty damn cute — stood up and extended his hand.

"Clark Van Wyck, what a pleasure."

"Janet Petrocelli, likewise."

"Please, have a seat. . . . So, I understand you have a family farm. That makes you a *hero* in my book. I've just introduced a bill called the Organic Initiative, which will provide a tax break to every organic farm in the state. I'm also working to exempt family farms from the state inheritance tax. We *need* to keep you folks in business. Linda tells me you're up in Delaware County. Whereabouts exactly?"

"It isn't *my* farm."

"Oh?"

"It's a farm I have an interest in — Kelly's Farm."

All the color drained from his face but this cat was quick and came right back, "I'm sorry, I don't know it."

"Are you sure?"

"Absolutely sure."

He looked at me and I got the distinct impression he was willing me to dematerialize. Must be all that yoga. Sorry, Charlie, no namaste.

"A friend of mine worked at Kelly's Farm," I said. "She's dead and I think she was murdered."

"I'm sorry to hear that." He picked his cellphone up off his desk, looked at it, put it back down. "Have you contacted the authorities?"

I wasn't taking that bait. "No."

He relaxed a bit, leaned back in his chair, and then leaned forward, solicitous. "It's always so hard to lose a friend."

"Her name was Natasha Wolfson, she died on Platte Clove eleven days ago."

"Oh yes, of course. That was very sad. I thought I read that her death has been ruled a suicide or an accident."

"It has."

"But you think it was murder?"

"I do."

"Do you have any evidence?"

"Did you know Natasha Wolfson?"

"No."

"Someone took a picture of your car parked at Kelly's Farm." This was true: I had *taken* a picture, no need to tell him it no longer existed.

He swallowed and then smiled, but looked a little sick around the gills. "I visit district farms as often as I can."

"Apparently you're a regular at this one. You were there two nights ago."

"You mean my *car* was."

One good bluff deserved another. "Actually, my sources tell me *you* were."

He leaned back, thinking, and then grew mock sorrowful. "Politics is a rough business. There are a lot of *unreliable* sources. It's always best to fact check yourself."

"That's why I'm here."

"I wish I could be of more help. The Platte Clove is very dangerous, there are deaths up there every year. There's been talk of putting up guardrails, but it's within the boundaries of Catskill Park so there are competing constituencies."

"The environmentalists versus the murderers?"

He stood up. "It's been a pleasure. I'm giving a speech on the Hudson Valley's water issues this evening so I'm pretty busy."

I glanced at the Tiffany's catalogue, "You look it."

He quickly closed it and pushed it aside, "My wife's birthday is coming up."

Thanks to the guilt factor, cheated-on wives always get better presents — I knew things were sliding downhill in my second marriage when the Asshole started bringing flowers home.

"Maybe you should give her the truth."

"The truth is rarely a popular gift."

"Oh, I'm always happy to get the truth, in fact I'm obsessive about it."

"Obsession can be dangerous."

"I've heard you're obsessed with becoming governor."

He laughed. "Don't believe everything you hear. I *do* have an agenda that I believe will benefit the people of this state."

"I hope justice is on it."

"Let me know if there's anything else I can do."

"You can stop lying."

Something cold and hard and terrifying flitted over his features. Then he smiled all toothy and boyish and said, "Politics has gotten so nasty these days. I want to change that."

I had an urge to slap that smile right off his face.

Then I remembered that he liked to get slapped.

Twenty-Seven

I left Albany and headed for Phoenicia. I needed to go back to Natasha's house, to see if there was anything I'd missed, any clue that would lead me deeper into her life and psyche, help me piece together the last months — and particularly the last night — of her life.

I parked on Phoenicia's main drag and tried to look casual as I sauntered up Natasha's street, all the while scanning to make sure I wasn't seen. I reached her bungalow and walked into its overgrown front yard like I belonged there. The front door was locked so I slipped in through the porch window again.

It was late afternoon and the living room was eerie in the dim filtered light, nothing had been moved, nothing changed — a wave of sadness swept over me, for Natasha, for all the hurt in the world.

But I had work to do.

I began a methodical search, looking under cushions, through closets, in corners and crannies. The living room yielded zip. There was a small dining area and I noticed a laptop in its case on the floor beside a cabinet — *that* was coming with me. I hit the kitchen, it looked like Natasha was a vegetarian but that was all I learned. There was a small pantry and I opened all the drawers and looked behind the cans of soup and boxes of oatmeal. Then I noticed a cookie tin on the top shelf. I pulled a chair into the pantry, stood on it and picked up the box. It rattled. I stepped down and opened it — a half dozen pill vials. Each contained a different pill. None of them had prescription labels. I took two pills from each vial, slipped them into a small baggie and then into my bag and replaced the tin.

I moved into the bedroom and noticed a bookshelf with a row of about a half dozen photo albums. I sat on the bed and leafed through them. They were in chronological order, starting when Natasha was about fourteen, the early pictures taken at what was obviously her boarding school. She was exuberant in some shots, hamming for the camera, hanging on friends, singing; in other shots she looked moody and troubled. Tellingly, there were few pictures of her parents or sister. The last album was filled with pictures of her life in Phoenicia: Natasha with Billie, singing in small clubs, playing in the snow.

Then at the end of the album I came to a manila envelope. Written on the front was: "Natasha — Here they are. Burn them. I am so sorry. I love you — P." I opened the envelope and took out a small pile of photographs. The first was a nude of Natasha taken on a large sleigh bed, a fetching shot of her on her side, propped on pillows, her body pale and voluptuous, her expression playful, teasing, seductive. In the pictures that followed she begins to look high on something — some downer with aphrodisiac properties, her poses increasingly explicit, her hair disheveled, her body flushed, her eyes hooded and filled with something more dangerous, yearning and sadness, a lost child playing a grown-up game.

Then I came to the nudes of Pavel in all his considerable glory, sprawled out on the same bed, looking straight into the lens with a beckoning satyr smile — there was nothing playful in his eyes, his sexual confidence was frightening — the man was pure sex, male sex, ruthless and insistent.

Then I came to the shots of them together, clearly taken the same day. The pictures were disturbing because in them they weren't making love, they were having sex, raw sex, you could almost smell the long afternoon of lust, sweat, commingled juices, in some shots their bodies were clearly posed, it was a performance directed by the photographer — whoever that was — Pavel's face filled with conquest and triumph, Natasha passive, groggy, drugged into submission and . . . was that fear I saw in her eyes? These pictures were about power, power over a vulnerable young woman.

As I put the pictures back in the envelope, the room, the world seemed very still. Natasha was unable to resist Pavel and was drawn into his heart of darkness — a kind, brave, gifted girl with a fierce core of sadness, insecurity, and self-hatred that she was constantly battling. Sometimes she won, sometimes she didn't. In the months before her death, she was losing.

I had to find out who took these shots.

Just then I heard a key in the front door. I slipped the photos into my bag, quickly replaced the albums and walked into the living room just as Sally Wolfson walked in the door. She looked exhausted, older, no make-up, and was carrying an empty satchel.

"Oh, hello," she said in surprise.

"Hi."

We eyed each other.

"I didn't expect to find anyone here," she said.

"You'll have to excuse me, I was snooping around."

"Why?"

"I don't think your daughter's death was an accident or a suicide."

"You mean . . . ?"

"I think she was murdered."

She closed her eyes and inhaled sharply. Then she exhaled with a sigh and sat on the sofa. When she spoke her voice was soft, "Why do you think that?"

"Because I was with her the day she died and she didn't seem suicidal to me. I'm a former therapist so I have some training."

She looked up at me, "But who would kill her?"

"That's what I'm trying to find out."

"Do you have any evidence that she was murdered?"

"I'm looking."

"The police investigated. My husband and I spoke with them. They ruled the cause of death undetermined."

"I think they're wrong."

She looked down at her lap for a long moment and finally looked up at me with red-rimmed eyes, "I don't know how much you know about my daughter, but she was troubled. The last few months have been very difficult for her. But at heart she was a lovely girl, as far as I know she didn't have any enemies."

"Did you meet her current boyfriend, Pavel?"

"Yes, once. Unbelievably handsome, but a real opportunist, I didn't think he was good for Natasha. Do you think *he* killed her?"

"I don't know."

She seemed to marshal herself, sat up straight, pushed her hair back. "As I'm sure you can imagine this has been very difficult for me and my husband. Our healing has just begun. A lot of wild speculation will only add to our pain."

"I understand, but I can't let a murderer get away with it."

"I appreciate your concern for Natasha. If and when you have any information to back up your theory, please contact us immediately." She stood up. "Now I came here today to pick up some of my daughter's things, just those that have some meaning for me and Howard."

"I'll leave you alone."

"Thank you."

I walked to the door and turned. "Oh, by

the way, I read about your book contract."

Her eyes opened wide for just a split second. "I suppose we seem guilty of opportunism, too. In fact, we've been writing the book for several years, and were desperately hoping for a happy ending, with Natasha successful again." Her voice caught. "But it wasn't meant to be."

I had a feeling there was more coming, so I waited.

"I know it might seem as if we're exploiting Natasha's death, but offers from publishers came in right away, the industry is so ruthless these days. We've turned down a dozen television requests — *60 Minutes,* Charlie Rose, Dr. Phil. It's just too soon."

I wondered what the expiration date was on "too soon." Another month maybe? I never quite got how people could go public with their private lives, but then again I'm not a celebrity. I think that in a funny way when you crave attention and live your life in the spotlight, you *need* it to validate your experiences, it's almost as if something hasn't really happened until you've gone public with it.

"Oh listen, Julia showed up at my shop and I gave her Natasha's jewelry. So I think we're square."

"You *gave* her the jewelry?"

I nodded.

"Oh dear. Julia is also going through a rough patch herself. And that jewelry was my husband's and my property."

"I realize that. But I did it. Do you want me to pay you, too?"

"No, of course not. I'm sorry for snapping. This hasn't been an easy time."

I wanted to feel more sympathy for Sally, but there was something cold about her — she seemed genuinely upset about Natasha's death but had spoken mainly about its effect on her and her husband, had said little about Natasha, not a memory, not a word of longing or loss. The death was something that was happening to *her,* which is the classic narcissistic response.

"That's okay. Listen, please give me a call if you ever want to talk." I handed her my card.

"Yes, and let us know if you turn up anything. If you do, we'll want to get involved, to help, to push." She looked around the small forlorn house. "Poor Natasha."

Sally's Mercedes was parked out front. I walked to my car and drove to the intersection of Natasha's street, where I had a view of the cottage gate. I turned on WDST and waited. About fifteen minutes later, Sally walked out, her satchel full. I pulled away and circled the block.

Then I parked, walked to Natasha's and slipped back inside. The laptop was still there. I picked it up. The place looked like it had been gone over pretty quickly; cupboards and closets were half open and disarranged, in the bedroom the photo albums were gone, in the pantry the pill tin was on a lower shelf. I opened it — empty.

Twenty-Eight

When I got home I set up Natasha's laptop on the kitchen table and turned it on. That was about as far as I got, me and computers not being on the best of terms. I called Josie and filled her in.

"She may have set her computer so that she just stayed signed in. If she did, we'll be able to access her mail — no prob. If not, things are going to get more complicated. So just click on her browser."

I did as I was told.

"What's her homepage?"

"Google."

"Now click on gmail on the upper right — fingers crossed."

Sure enough, Natasha's e-mail account popped up.

"Wow, that was easy. Thanks."

"Anytime."

I methodically read all of her recent e-mails. There were very few since her death, mostly adverts and offers. In the weeks before her death there were short messages from her friend Vondra in LA on the mechanics of her move and general gossip, and from several people in the music business who she was connecting with as she prepared to move. There was nothing from Clark Van Wyck or Kelly, but they were probably too discreet to use email. There were several from Pavel, including this one sent a week before her death:

"Baby — I am SO sorry for what happen yesterday. Pls forgive Pavel, he loves you."

That must refer to the photos.

Scrolling down to a couple of weeks earlier, there was this one from Pavel:

"I have more of what you want, see you later. I love you love you — P"

'More of what you want'? Could that be the pills? Was Pavel her pill connection?

Then I read a series of e-mails from Sally Wolfson that had come in during the last month of Natasha's life:

"Darling Tosh-Tosh — I'm worried about you. Pls answer when I call. Are you all right? We want to help, pls let us in — xxoo mom."

"Baby girl — you didn't sound like yourself on the phone yesterday. If there's ANYTHING you need, pls pls pls call us.

Love you so much xxoo mom."

"Darling girl — I know you're having a hard time right now, but please let's talk about it. CALL ME. You've gotten through worse. Be strong and know how much we love you — xxoo mom."

This one came in just two days before Natasha's death:

"Natasha — why are you cutting us off like this? Are you definitely moving to LA? We're SO worried about you and love you so much. We want to be part of your life, my sweet-voiced angel. Sending SO much love to my cutie kitten xxoo mom."

I got up and poured myself a cup of coffee. If Pavel was Natasha's pill connection, it raised a lot of questions. Where was he getting the pills? And why was he supplying Natasha if he loved her? Why did he go along with the photo session? Was he just a psychopath or was he doing someone else's bidding?

And Sally's e-mails seemed sincere enough, but the tone and use of pet names were infantilizing and the offers of help were general and vague. You'd think a professional like Sally would supply names of doctors and therapists, and specific offers of financial help or to pay for treatment.

Natasha led a very complicated life.
And so, increasingly, did I.

Twenty-Nine

It was late the next afternoon and George was sitting at my kitchen table identifying the pills I'd found at Natasha's. Afterwards we were going to head down to Mad John's — this was Goat Island night. I can't say I was looking forward to it. The theft of Indian artifacts didn't seem as important as uncovering the truth of Natasha's death, but Mad John and George were the valley's protectors and I was proud to enlist.

"This is oxycodone, which is basically heroin in pill form, I mean these suckers will turn you into a zombie."

I thought of the explicit photographs and wondered if this was the pill Natasha was on when they were taken.

George picked up another pill, "This is Adderall, which takes you in the other direction — it's pure speed and unlike a lot of speed, it can make you *very* horny. Here we have Vicodin, a serious painkiller and downer. Two of these and you are gone for the foreseeable future. Xanax, no introduction needed, some people pop these like M&Ms, they're great for coming down from a speed run. This baby here is Ritalin, which will treat your ADHD and also turn you into a jaw-twitching paranoid speed freak. If Natasha was taking all of these she was pouring a lot of chemicals into her body, all of them reacting to each other, doing herself some serious damage. Did she seem whacked that day you met her?"

"She was emotional, high-strung, too up, but she was making sense, I didn't feel like I was talking to some drug casualty. Is it hard to get a hold of these pills?"

"It's not easy, you can get them on the street if you know where and how. Scrips are the easiest, of course, but most of these drugs are tightly controlled and monitored so doctors are very careful about over-prescribing. You don't know where Natasha was getting them?"

"I think from Pavel, but I'm not sure. I've got my work cut out for me."

"Speaking of which, it's time for our next assignment."

Thirty

George and I collected our sleeping bags and the picnic basket Abba had packed for us, and drove down to the lighthouse parking lot. We made our way to Mad John's lair and found him pacing in circles, looking worried.

"What's up, man?" George asked.

"Bad moon rising."

"Should we go another night?"

"No! We have to go tonight. They'll come tonight, I'm sure of it."

"Listen," I said, "If they do come, I don't think we should do anything rash. The important thing is to identify them, not apprehend them. That's the police's job."

Mad John and George exchanged a look.

"I mean it, guys."

We made our way to Mad John's mooring, a muddy little inlet in the riverbank where he tethered his raft to a gnarly old tree. He pulled the raft close to shore,

George and I clambered aboard — it was a surprisingly sturdy craft, made of driftwood and other scavenged debris. Mad John untied us, leapt onboard, and pushed us off with his long oar.

We made our way down the river, close to shore, the air a hazy bluish gray in the falling twilight, the river rippled by a gentle breeze, the raft rocking, the earthy wet smell, the September air warm but not heavy with humidity. Now that we were out on the river Mad John seemed to relax, he started to hum softly. I lay down with my hands behind my head, George joined me, we watched the sky darken above us.

"You okay, Janet?" he asked in an intimate voice.

"Yeah, just a little obsessed with Natasha."

"Murder is weird, isn't it?"

"What is it that allows a person to go from wanting someone dead to actually planning and carrying out their murder? They have to just shut down some part of themselves, their conscience, their morality, it's an incredible act of denial, almost a form of willful insanity."

"I think what stops a lot of people isn't right or wrong, it's fear of being caught," George said. "If people thought they could get away with it, there would be *a lot* more murder. Where I think the denial comes in, is that people delude themselves into thinking they won't get caught."

"Good point. So there are two denials going on at the same time."

"Yeah. So you really think Natasha was murdered?"

"I'm sure leaning that way. A lot of people wanted her out of the picture. It's just figuring out who had that weird psychological ability — and the sheer will and drive — to take it from thought to action."

We were quiet for a minute, Mad John was still humming softly, and in his hum I heard his love for the river. The first stars were growing visible; I wished Josie was with us.

"What was your mom like, George?" I asked.

"Oh, she was pretty great. She was pure Brooklyn Irish, tough and sentimental. After my dad died she worked two jobs — it wasn't easy. Of course she liked her whiskey, and a man now and then. There were five of us kids and Friday nights were everyone's favorite, school and work were over, she'd pour herself a glass of whiskey, put opera on the record player, and make us dinner of baked potato, Le Sueur baby peas from that silver can, and frozen fish sticks. We'd all sit around the table laughing and talking, then she'd shoo us kids out to the street to play. I think she liked being alone with her whiskey, her opera, and her memories."

"Did you come out to her?"

"When you grow up on the streets of Bay Ridge, there are no secrets. I told her when I was thirteen."

"What did she say?"

" 'I don't give a shit'."

"Sweet and simple."

"Yeah. She loved me good, Janet. You know, she lived to see us all out of house, on our own, I think she was proud of that."

"Time to cross the river," Mad John said.

I loved watching as he deftly oared us across the river like a gallant gondolier. There wasn't another boat in sight and in the dusky light it felt like we were rowing into a dream.

We reached Goat Island, it came to a rocky tip but otherwise looked pretty much like the rest of the shoreline. There was a low rock shelf and Mad John steered us to it. He hopped off, grabbed his rope, and pulled the raft close. George and I stepped onto the island with our gear and then Mad John hauled the raft onto land and into a thicket, out of sight.

"Follow me," he said.

He knew the island well, we clambered up

a narrow path to reach the rocky spine. We came to a large clearing pocked with holes that looked recently dug and hastily filled. Mad John stopped and looked around sadly. "This is a sacred spot." He closed his eyes, held up his hands, and did a few rounds of gibberish chanting, no doubt invoking Native American spirits — and maybe Insane River Rat spirits, too.

After a bit, he shook himself out of his mini-trance, "Come on." He led us a little ways through some straggly woods until we came to a large rock outcropping. He led us around the side and there was a cave. He ducked inside and we followed.

It was low-ceilinged, dark and dank, slithery and creepy and . . . *yuk.* Sleeping here would feel like sleeping inside a fish.

"Home sweet home," Mad John said with his first smile of the day.

"Can't we just sleep outside?" I suggested.

"No! The thieves might spot us and retreat. This way we can hear them and surprise them!"

George, ever practical in spite of himself, had already begun to lay out our sleeping bags and make a little nest. Mad John lit a couple of candles and before I knew it there was something Huck Finny and romantic about being in the cave. Sort of.

We had a nice picnic dinner thanks to Abba, sang *Bye Bye Blackbird* and a few other standards, and by then it was pitch dark.

"Time to wait," Mad John said, blowing out the candles.

I crawled into my sleeping bag and tried to ignore the lumpy-bumpy terrain under me. No luck. I mean, isn't the whole point of evolution so that we *don't* have to sleep on the ground? The idea of doing it voluntarily just seems so . . . regressive. It was going to be a long night.

But we were here on a mission and these were my buds so I resigned myself to the situation. As my eyes got used to the dark, I saw that the walls of the cave were glistening and there were large bugs crawling on them. Yippee.

"Are you okay?" George whispered.

"Oh sure, I love spending the night inside Moby Dick's bile duct."

"Zen it out. But I mean are you *okay* okay? You seem distracted these days."

"George, I'm cold, clammy, my hip is pulsing with pain, and this place is Bugapalooza, I'm in no mood to get all deep."

There was a moment of silence and then he asked, "How'd it go with Josie up in Troy?"

"Will you and Abba back the fuck off about Josie, please?"

"Shhhhh!" Mad John hissed in a fury.

George smiled at me like a third grader admonished in class, I had to smile back. If Mad John had been my homeroom teacher, I probably would have done better in third grade.

Then we heard it — a scraping sound, a boat being pulled out of the water, onto the island's rocky shore. Mad John motioned us up to the front of the cave and started up a series of birdcalls; some avian amigos answered him. I quickly realized what he was doing — making noise to cover our movements.

Peering out from the mouth of the cave, I made out — through the brush and trees — the dim beam of a flashlight moving up from the river toward the clearing.

Mad John led us slowly out of the cave, all the while carrying on his birdcalls. We inched closer to the clearing from one direction as the beam of the flashlight approached from another. When we were about ten feet from the edge of the clearing Mad John motioned us to stop and crouch, hidden in the brush. My mouth was dry, my heart pounding so loudly in my chest I was afraid the thief would hear it. I took out my phone to take pictures.

The beam appeared at the edge of the clearing. It was impossible to make out the person holding it. Then the flashlight was placed in the crook of a tree branch, its beam shining down on the clearing. It was a man, a tall young man dressed all in black, his face hard to distinguish. He was carrying a shovel and he began to pace around the clearing, looking for a place to dig.

Then, as my eyes adjusted to the light, I realized who it was.

He stuck his shovel in the ground.

Mad John cocked his head: time to make our move. I shook my head "no," an adamant desperate "no." I had bigger fish to fry than the theft of artifacts. Mad John looked at me, uncomprehending. I raised my camera and took a shot. The flash lit up the clearing, the thief looked up in shock, I took another picture. He fled, crashing through the brush.

"Let him go!"

"No!" Mad John said, taking off in pursuit. I lunged and tackled him, we rolled around on the ground, he managed to get out of my grasp, but it was too late to catch the thief, we heard oars splashing in the river.

"What the fuck!!" an enraged Mad John

demanded.

"I'm sorry but I had to do that. That kid won't be back after that scare, he knows we're on to him. And these pictures are going to help me catch Natasha's killer."

"How?" George asked.

"Trust me."

Mad John and George gathered around as I pulled up the pictures of Collier Denton's "handyman," Graham.

Thirty-One

The next morning I went over to Chow for breakfast and hung out in the kitchen while Abba cooked, I always got a kick out of watching her, she was like an athlete or a dancer. The place was even more crowded than usual.

"Is there something going on in town?" I asked.

"Not that I know of."

I filled her in on what had happened on Goat Island and how I planned on using the photographs to force a little more information out of Collier Denton, who I was going to visit later in the day.

George rushed into the restaurant clutching a copy of the day's *New York Times.* He stopped in the middle of the place and let out a deafening, *"Hallelujah!"*

Abba smiled at me and said, "Somebody got laid last night." Then she stuck her head through the pass-through, "Take it down a notch, George, it's too early in the day."

"So you haven't seen it?" he asked.

"Seen what?"

He headed into the kitchen and folded opened the paper. "There's an article on the Hudson Valley in today's *Times.* Listen to this: 'In one of those serendipitous finds that makes travel writing so rewarding, I happened upon Chow, an unpretentious eatery in the village of Sawyerville. The setting and ambience are down home with a dose of quirk, and the food is nothing less than a revelation. My BLT redefined the classic with fresh-grated horseradish and herb-crusted local bacon on rye toast that could barely contain its multitude of caraway seeds. My lunchmate went into raptures over her sage-flecked chicken potpie, and as for the coconut-pecan-blackberry cake, well, heaven can wait.' "

Abba burst into a grin. Now Abba is not the grinning sort so when they do come, well, the world lights up.

"This calls for a party," she said. "Saturday night. Here."

"You are definitely going to need more help around the place," I said.

"I'm counting on *you* for that," she answered with a sly grin.

"We'll see."

"I gotta run, chicklets. Antonio is putting me on a real *fullsize* horse this morning!" George said.

"That's great, where?" I asked.

"Stop condescending to me."

"All I said was 'where'."

"As soon as I bring up the love of my life, you reduce me to some drooling obsessive."

"Well, George, this isn't the first time I've seen you in this infatuated state."

"Infatuated state? You're reducing my passion to an *infatuated state?* Abba, will you please inform Janet that our friendship is officially over, and that I never want to see or speak to her again."

Abba nodded.

George puffed himself up and added, "Now I'm going to go and mount Bingo."

"Wait a minute, isn't Bingo the thirty-two-year-old horse that lives at the Catskill Farm Animal Sanctuary?" Abba asked. "The one that's blind, deaf, and barely ambulatory?"

Pearl appeared at the pass-through to pick up an order.

"Pearl, will you please inform Abba that I am no longer speaking to her," George said. With that he turned and marched out the door.

Abba and I smiled at each other. A young couple came in, clutching the *Times*.

"Get ready for the deluge."

"Remember: I need your help."

"Yeah-yeah."

"And do you still want to work the Clark Van Wyck fundraiser tonight?"

"I do. What do you think of him?"

"You know, he seems on the up-and-up to me. He's from an old Valley family with not much money left, but his wife, Alice, has serious bucks. So he's too rich to be a hack, he really loves the Valley, and his green mania seems sincere. That wife is another story."

"Oh?"

"She's the power behind that carbon footprint. She's one of these *noblesse oblige* liberal types — it's her family money that's bankrolling him and she's *very* tough and savvy. She's the one who hired the fancy downstate talent that came up with the *New* New York thing. Hey, I kinda like the old New York. I don't trust her as far as I can asana."

I took all this in. "Yeah, I *definitely* want to work that fundraiser."

Thirty-Two

When I got home I called Chevrona.

"Has the stream been searched?" I asked.

"I put in the request and pushed pretty hard, but I don't think it's going to happen. Everyone is confident this was an accident or a suicide, and with our budget cuts . . ."

"Are *you* confident?"

There was a pause. "You're very persuasive, Janet. I'll push a little harder."

I wasn't going to wait. I put on my hiking boots and me and Sputnik drove to the bottom of the Platte Clove. I parked on the side of the road, we walked into the woods until we reached the Plattekill and set off alongside its bank. I was determined to walk up the gorge just in case some piece of evidence had fallen into the stream and been washed down.

The Platte Clove gorge is some of the most rugged terrain in the East, an awesome and kind of terrifying place. In the late nineteenth century it was a tourist attraction, on postcards and in guidebooks, with a wooden staircase that snaked up from the valley floor to the mountaintop. When Catskill Park was established, the staircase was torn down and these days access to the bottom of the clove is tricky, there isn't much parking and you have to cross private land.

Sputs and I made our way along the stream. It was pretty dramatic as the land climbed and narrowed, soon the stream was a steep fifty feet down. I hugged the trail, which at one point narrowed to not much more than a foot across. Then it flattened out and we were next to the stream again. Sputnik leapt in and took a quick swim. We passed a group of teenagers drinking beer and smoking pot — it's nice to know some things never change.

Pretty soon we were passing one amazing waterfall after another, large pools, with ancient rocks worn down into swirly patterns by eons of water, the gorge rising on either side. The higher we got the more vertical the walls got, I could see the sunlight on the treetops above, but none reached down into the dark heart of the clove. This was a narrow ravine and it was scary, a flash flood would have swept us to a watery death, bouncing us off the boulders. If we ran into a mass murderer there would be nowhere to run. Or an escaped mental patient. Or just some perv. None of this seemed to bother Sputnik in the least, he was in his glory racing around, leaping into the water, grabbing sticks.

I walked slowly, scouring the pools and both banks for any hint of color, any unusual shape or object, anything of Natasha's or her killer's that might have been swept downstream. I'd heard that there was a virtually inaccessible stretch below the pool where Natasha died. After about thirty minutes of hiking, we reached it. The rock walls rose straight up, the trail ended.

I stopped on a flattop boulder that jutted out over a small deep pool and looked up at the imposing rock walls, the only sound was the rushing stream and the wind rustling the tops of the trees. This was a lonely place. I imagined Natasha's last moments, as she was pushed into the void and plunged through the air toward the rocks below. Did she have time to feel fear? Or was she so drugged up that little registered, that she just let go?

Sputnik had made his way down to the pool and was splashing around.

"I think this is the end of the line for us,

Sputs." I sat down on the rock, took off my hiking boots, rolled up my pants legs and dangled my feet in the water. It was *cold* — cascading right down from its mountaintop spring — but I liked the jolt, it was refreshing and real, sort of an instant psychic cleansing. Natasha's death was proving complicated and draining on so many levels, I felt like I was being pulled into a lot of other people's lives and losing sight of my own. I needed this: the cold, the waterfall, the rock face dotted with iridescent patches of moss, the swaying green far above, I'm not the type to get mushy about nature, but sometimes it's just what a body needs — I inhaled the air, which was like nectar, and felt my blood pressure drop.

Sputnik had other ideas. He galumphed around the edge of the pool and up onto the boulder, proudly holding a cellphone in his mouth.

Thirty-Three

I tried to turn the phone on but it was dead. Could it be revived? I wanted to get it to Chevrona ASAP. Sputnik and I made our way back down the gorge. A little ways past the teenagers, two men appeared on the trail, heading toward us. One was big, beefy, hulking, the other lean, wiry, coiled; they looked very backcountry, unshaven funky in dirty jeans, t-shirts, and baseball caps. The closer they got, the less I liked the vibe — these two weren't out on a nature hike. My muscles went tense, Sputnik sensed it and tensed up, too.

The trail narrowed up ahead and they stopped there and waited, blocking the way. We reached them.

"Excuse us," I said.

"Ah, maybe not," the big guy said. They laughed.

"You boys have something you want to say to me?"

The little one turned to the big one, "I don't know, we got something we want to say to her?"

"Duh, let me think."

Sputnik's hair was up and he let out a low growl.

"Very amusing, I'm sure, but we need to get past," I said.

"What you *need* is to understand that you're fucking around where you don't belong," the wiry one said.

"Who sent you?"

"Kelly sent us," he said, "She said to tell you this is her second warning. Three strikes and you're out."

"Yeah, back off or else."

"Or else what?"

"Or else this," the big one said, kicking Sputnik in the chest. The poor guy wailed, flew through the air, and collapsed on the ground.

I pivoted and kicked my foot up under the wiry one's chin, *hard,* sending him flying into a tree. His head smashed into the trunk and he crumpled to the ground. The big guy lunged at me, I ducked, spun around, and nailed him face-on with my right fist — it hurt me more than him but it bought me enough time to plant myself and kick him in the gut. Hard. Twice. He went down and curled on his side. Blood was pouring out of the wiry guy's mouth, he spit out a tooth and what looked like a piece of his tongue.

"Either of you assholes ever touch my dog again — or *any* dog, or any *animal* for that matter — and I'll rip your heads off and go bowling with them. You got that?"

When they hesitated I kicked the big one in the side of his head. "I asked you a question, dickwad."

"I got it," he mumbled.

I took a step toward the wiry one.

"I got it," he blubbered.

Sputnik was back on his feet — tough little mutter — by my side, looking a little woozy but crouched and growling.

"Tell Kelly I have a message for her: I don't give a shit what goes down at her farm, but if one of her customers is a murderer I'm going to bring him in. I'd advise her to work *with* me on this. Come on, Sputs."

As we walked away, Sputnik licked my hand.

It's nice to feel appreciated.

Thirty-Four

I drove home, with a quick stop to pick up a nice filet mignon for Sputs, who seemed to have no memory of his trauma but certainly enjoyed the steak. After calling to make sure she was there, I headed down to the New York State Police barracks on Route 209 to give the phone to Chevrona. I found the detective in her office, surrounded by papers. She stood up as I walked in — what a gentlewoman.

"Is this a bad time?"

"I'm pretty swamped, but . . . no." She smiled that knowing little smile of hers.

What was it about being in the same room with Chevrona that just made me feel better about being alive?

I handed her the phone, she immediately took out the batteries. "You did excellent work here."

"Do you think you'll be able to retrieve anything?"

"Depends how long this was in the water. The shorter the better, obviously. It's damp but not dripping, which is a good sign. My guess is Sputnik found it on the bank."

"How long will it take to find out?"

"I'll ask the lab to expedite, but since the death hasn't been classified a homicide, probably a week at least."

I considered mentioning my little dustup with Mutt and Jeff but decided I should keep that side of the investigation to myself for now.

"Hey listen, Abba is having a party Saturday night to celebrate this amazing write-up she got in the *Times*. Any chance you could drop by?"

She looked at me and squinted — I went a little jello-y in the knees.

"I'll do my best."

From there I headed straight down to Stone Ridge. I needed to talk to Pavel and the pictures I'd found at Natasha's place gave me some new leverage. I'd photographed them with my cell to protect the originals and to take denial off the table.

I turned down the drive at Bumpland — there was a horde of gardeners around — and headed straight for the garage. Pavel's motorcycle was outside. I parked and went inside to find the door up to his garret locked. He must be in the main house. I took a deep breath and headed over there.

One of the myriad maids answered the door. She had a feather duster in one hand and a cellphone in the crook of her neck, ". . . *segundo,*" she said before looking me up and down, "What you want?"

"I'm looking for Pavel. Is he around?"

She waved her feather duster in the general direction of the sunroom and then turned and walked away, resuming her chat.

I walked through the formal rooms with their priceless antiques and walls covered with Octavia's splatter art. I reached the sunroom to find Octavia, Pavel, and a coifed-to-the-nines middle-aged woman sitting around the table with all sorts of booklets, swatches, and catalogues spread out in front of them.

"I can get you Kim Kardashian, but her price is $250,000," the woman said.

"Oh my goodness, look who's here!" Octavia cried when she saw me. She leapt from her chair and raced over, taking my hands in hers. "Ciao-shalom! A pop visit! How marvelous! How American!"

"Hi, Pavel," I said.

"Hello," he said, his eyes flashing triumph.

The woman gave me a big blazing smile, "How do you do. I'm Lauren Parker-

Lipschitz."

"Oh dear, forgive me, I'm so giddy with all this wedding planning that I've quite forgotten my manners. Never mind."

Pavel certainly hadn't been wasting time. Suddenly the pictures carried new power — and risk.

"Janet, what do *you* think of Patti LaBelle?" Octavia asked.

"I think she's a fantastic performer."

"Oh, I *knew* you would, you're so simpatico. I can just hear her wailing 'Here Comes the Bride' in four octaves. We're having a *Buddhist* ceremony. I forget why. Let's have some champagne! Delores, dear," she called in the direction of the kitchen, "bring us a bottle of champagne! . . . Come, sit down." I joined them at the table. "Pavel wants Lady Gaga, but I think she's awfully showy."

"She's also ten times as expensive as LaBelle," Lauren Parker-Lipschitz said.

Octavia waved her hand in dismissal, "Oh bish-bosh, don't bother me about money."

Parker-Lipschitz eyes flashed dollar signs.

A maid brought in the champagne and four flutes on a tray. Pavel deftly opened the bottle and poured the bubbly. He handed a flute to Octavia, who gave a quivery shudder when their hands touched. "Oh, *thank you,* my darling."

"To the blissful couple," Parker-Lipschitz said, raising her glass.

We all clinked.

"When's the happy day?" I asked.

"October 23rd! Rasputin the Fabulous, my phone psychic, picked it! Oh, he went on for *hours* about omens and energy and vibrations! Vera Wang is doing my dress. At first she demurred but then I sent her a blank check. I've only made one stipulation: *no panties!* My vagina would never speak to me again." She leaned across the table and kissed Pavel, he returned the kiss and before you know it there some serious tongue action happening.

I shot Parker-Lipschitz a glance, but she wasn't going to mock this meal ticket and ignored me, beaming in an *oh-you-lovebirds* way.

The betrothed couple showed no inclination to stop their necking. In fact, Octavia was practically up on the table, running her fingers through Pavel's hair, down his neck, moaning.

A maid walked by the doorway and muttered, "Puta."

Octavia was sucking on Pavel's tongue and her body was starting to quiver.

"I love England," Parker-Lipschitz said to

fill the awkward void. Octavia took one of Pavel's hands and placed it on her ample bosom. "It has so much class and decorum."

Octavia was now up on the table, on all fours, crawling across it toward Pavel, making weird growling noises.

"Have you been to England yourself, Janet?" Parker-Lipschitz asked, a growing edge in her voice.

"Once."

"I can't get enough of the royal family."

Octavia made it across the table and slithered onto Pavel's lap. She unbuttoned his shirt and started to lick his muscular chest.

Parker-Lipschitz's voice flew up to falsetto. "I collect Princess Anne memorabilia."

Octavia had Pavel's shirt off and was sucking on one of his nipples.

"What the bloody hell is going on here?!" Lavinia boomed, walking into the room. She was wearing Wellingtons and men's tweed hunting attire, an identically dressed Jerome perched on her shoulder.

"Oh hello!" Parker-Lipschitz cried in relief, leaping to her feet. "I'm Lauren Parker-Lipschitz, Octavia's wedding planner. You must be her brother." She took in Jerome and her mouth fell open.

Out the picture window a delirious maid

ran by, followed by a gardener in hot pursuit.

"I am indeed, Vin Bump, what a pleasure. And this is Jerome. I'm afraid he's in a mood, his hypoglycemia is acting up." She pulled out a flask and took a deep pull, then noticed her sister. "For God's sake, Octavia, rein in your id!"

Octavia looked up from her suckling, lipstick smeared all over her face. She blinked her eyes, like she was coming back to reality, and looked at us all as if for the first time. "Oh, goodness, did I get a touch carried away? No matter."

"My dear girl, you look like a clown who lost her circus," Vin said. "Women are so vexing."

Parker-Lipschitz sat up straight and clapped her hands together, trying to get control of things, "We still haven't settled on a *theme* for the wedding."

"Do I look a fright?" Octavia asked Pavel.

"You look like love," he answered.

Octavia moaned.

"The *theme* pulls the wedding together — you know, unity, the circle of life, *hakuna matata.*"

"Carmelita, bring Jerome a steak and kidney pie!" Vin called in the direction of the kitchen.

"Joy, or as the French like to say *joie,* comes to mind," Parker-Lipschitz suggested.

"Do let me go freshen up," Octavia said, pulling herself off Pavel's lap and walking a bit unsteadily out of the room.

Time to move. Fast.

I stood up, "Pavel, could I talk to you for a second?" He smirked. "It's about some photographs . . . of you and Natasha." The smirk disappeared.

Pavel followed me out of the room.

"Joy is modern *and* eternal and . . . *joyous!*" Parker-Lipschitz cried to her dwindling audience.

"What in the bloody hell are you blathering on about!?" Vin demanded.

As soon as we were in the adjoining library I whipped out my camera and pulled up one of the more explicit pictures, "Who took this?" He hesitated. "Maybe I'll just ask the US immigration service. Octavia will be heartbroken when you're deported, but she'll get over it — there are a lot of Pavels in the sea."

Pavel exhaled in surrender. "Collier."

"Collier took the pictures, at his house?"

"Yes."

"Nastasha was taking a lot of pills. Do you know where she was getting them?"

"From Collier."

"Bullshit."

"He gave them to me to give to her."

"And you did it?"

"He threatened me like you just did, with deportation."

"Why did he want her on pills?"

"He wanted her sick, so he could have me all for him." He couldn't resist a smug little smile.

"So you fed her drugs. What an upstanding guy."

"I did not kill her."

"Did Collier?"

"I don't know."

Octavia appeared, "What are you two tete-a-teteing about?" She threw her arms around Pavel's neck. "Keep your hands off my man, young lady, or I'll have to murder you, too!"

Parker-Lipschitz popped her head into the room, "Are we feeling the *joie?*"

THIRTY-FIVE

I headed right over to Collier Denton's place. He answered the door wearing that same dressing gown, took one look at me, and said, "What do *you* want?"

"Answers from *you.*"

I showed him a picture of Graham digging on Goat Island. His coloring grew even more sepulchral, but he came back with, "That picture means nothing to me."

"I wonder if it would mean something to the police?"

There was a long pause and then he exhaled with a deep sigh, the fight seeming to leak out of him, at least momentarily.

"What do you want?"

"I want to know who killed Natasha Wolfson."

He looked over at Bumpland, his eyes filled with a mix of suspicion, rage, and longing. Then he turned and walked into his house, leaving the door open. I followed through the half-furnished rooms and into his study. He sat in his wing chair — surrounded by the detritus and essentials of his life. I remained standing.

"You could at least have brought a bottle of champagne," he said, like a petulant child.

"I'll make you a deal — you level with me, I'll buy you the bubbly."

"Veuve?"

"Sure."

"You're smart."

"Dogged maybe."

"Pavel is over there right now, isn't he?"

I wanted to play these characters off of each other, get each one suspicious of the other, thinking I knew more than I actually did.

"Yes, he is. He and Octavia are planning their wedding."

A little involuntary cry escaped him. It was almost touching. Then his mouth curled in disgust. "The little shit. I *made* him. . . . Do you want to know the worst part?"

I nodded.

"I still want him back. More than anything in the world. Believe it or not, my blackened heart can still love."

I didn't believe it.

"Pavel told me about the drugs."

He waved a hand in dismissal, his sleeve rode up, revealing that ill-concealed burn scar on his forearm, "That was a *good* deed. He told me she was having trouble sleeping, so I sent along an oxy. Arrest me."

"Oxy and Vicodin and Adderall and Xanax and Ritalin."

"One thing led to another."

"You wanted her dead."

"And I got my wish."

"Where did you get the drugs?"

He seemed taken aback, but just for a blink, and then smiled slyly, "I have my sources. At my age, you know, one *accumulates* things. Including obliging doctors who understand how *trying* old age can be."

I pulled up one of the sex photos. "Why did you take this?"

He looked mildly shocked for a moment. "Those were for my personal pleasure."

"That's pretty sick."

"I am what I am."

"A murderer?"

He laughed. "Only in my dreams."

"Is there arson in your dreams?"

His mouth dropped open and he tipped back in his chair as if pushed by an invisible hand, but recovered in a breath, "Have you taken leave of your senses?"

"That scar on your arm . . . Ian Stock dies in a tragic fire. You're hired to replace him."

"That was all in another lifetime. Ian was a *dear* friend of mine, a fearful alcoholic, his death was caused by an errant Winston." His confidence restored, he grew cavalier, "As for this scar, *never* try to make banana flambé after four martinis. Now *that* was a memorable dinner party." He laughed, a little too loudly.

Graham walked into the room wearing nothing but a jockstrap and carrying a can of beer. He had a muscular body, one that looked like it had been earned in hard time, not the gym. And the tattoos that spread across his arms and torso had that primitive done-in-prison look.

"Not now, darling, I've got company."

"W'ever," he mumbled.

"Wait a second." I showed him the picture on Goat Island. "You take a nice picture."

He actually smiled and said, "Eh, thanks." Then it sunk in. "That was you?"

I nodded.

His jaw set, his black eyes turned to hard coal, he reached for the camera, I stepped back.

"There are other copies, so cool it."

He looked over at Denton, made fists, bounced on his heels.

"She wins, I'm afraid."

"I want every stolen artifact returned. Drop them off at the State Police Barracks on 209, attention of Detective Chevrona Williams. Got that?"

Denton nodded wearily. His none-too-bright thug-du-jour still looked like he wanted to take me out.

"We'll talk," I said, turning to leave.

"Wait. I leveled with you, now where's my Veuve?"

"You get that when I get the *whole* truth."

It was a bluff but, hey, champagne ain't cheap.

Thirty-Six

It was later that evening, and I was helping Abba get ready for the Clark Van Wyck fundraiser. We were in an open-sided tent on the grounds of Opus 40, which is one of the crown jewels of the Hudson Valley. Set a few miles outside Sawyerville, it's an *amazing* six-acre outdoor sculpture made entirely of native bluestone, with pools, walkways, ramps, all centered around a central monolith. The site had originally been a quarry and sculptor Harvey Fite built the whole shebang without mortar, using old quarrymen tools and techniques. It was his passion and lifework, and he dubbed it Opus 40 because he figured it would take forty years to finish. The place has a sad and ironic coda: in 1976, in year thirty-seven of forty, Fite was killed in an accident as he worked on the project.

It was a gorgeous evening, warm and dry, and in the distance the Catskills rose up from the valley. The Van Wyck campaign was expecting about two hundred people so Abba had hired some local kids to help out. It wasn't a sit-down, so she was serving hors d'oeuvrey things like individual quiches, bacon-wrapped figs, various small kabobs. As usual, just about all the food was local. A jazz trio was setting up, and a couple of campaign aides were bustling about tacking up "Building A *New* New York" banners.

The guests were going to start arriving in about forty-five minutes and I was putting out platters on a long table. A tall, fit woman in her late thirties strode into the tent — no make-up, great bone structure, wearing elegant slacks, a drapey silk blouse, and a narrow belt. She radiated money, intelligence, drive, and looked like she spent half her life in vigorous athletic pursuits and the other half making the rest of us feel inadequate about ourselves.

She strode over to me, "Alice Van Wyck. Are you in charge?"

"No, that would be Abba," I said, pointing in her direction.

She walked over to Abba, pointed to the plastic forks and knives and asked, "Are these utensils biodegradable?"

"I don't know," Abba said.

"You *don't know?*"

Abba shook her head.

"We can't use them then," Van Wyck said, throwing up her hands in frustration, then muttering under her breath, "I have to do *everything* myself."

"I don't think we've got time to replace them," Abba said, keeping her cool.

"Melanie?!" Van Wyck called to a young woman outside the tent. Melanie, who looked about nineteen and was wearing a power suit, ran in, a look of foreboding on her face. "Did you check to make sure the utensils were biodegradable?"

Melanie flinched and said, "I'm sorry."

"Do you know what my husband stands for?"

"A better, stronger, greener New York, a *New* New York."

"That's right — a *greener* New York! He has enemies *everywhere* — there will probably be opp research people here this evening. Can you *imagine* what will happen if this gets out? It will be spread all over *The Post,* YouTube, Hannity, right-wing blogs, it will be a *debacle.*" Her voice was rising and her color right along with it. "This is just the kind of mistake that can *destroy* a career these days! I want you to go find us two hundred biodegradable knives, forks, and spoons. *Right now!*"

Melanie looked like she was about to cry.

"Most of this is finger food, I don't think —" Abba began.

"Is the *salad* finger food?" Van Wyck demanded.

"Obviously not, but I don't think we need two hundred —"

"You're being paid to provide the food, not to think."

"Would you please let me finish?"

Van Wyck reared back like a startled horse, rendered momentarily speechless.

Abba took advantage of that moment, "Let me call a friend in town, he should be able to help us out." She had her cell out and punched in a number. "Hey, George, it's Abba, I know you're coming to the fundraiser, but can you possibly head over to Chow, grab as much silverware as you can and bring it all out to us right now?" She lowered her voice, "It's a red-alert situation. . . . You're a doll." She hung up. "He'll be here in about fifteen minutes with more than enough to get us through."

"Are you *sure?*"

"No, I just said it to mess with your head."

Van Wyck's mouth dropped open, incredulous. "This is the last time you work for us."

"I could have told *you* that," Abba said.

Van Wyck narrowed her eyes, gauging the

situation. Then she came to a decision, gave a little shrug of dismissal, and walked out of the tent. "Someone is *not* getting it at home," Abba said.

"Ain't that the truth," I said.

Melanie tried to suppress her smile.

The crowd had an educated/artsy upper-middle-class look — lots of long flowing clothes on the women, who all looked like they got weekly massages and read the latest books. The men were a mix of the lean and well-fed look — jeans with oxford shirts and loosened ties — and laid-back Woodstock types with bellies, cool shirts worn loose, and sandals. While the waiters passed trays, Abba and I stood behind the main serving table. George was nearby, regaling a small clutch of listeners with a somewhat exaggerated version of the Goat Island story. Clark and Alice Van Wyck made their separate ways through the crowd, working it full tilt.

"Those two are slick," she said.

"And a little creepy, don't you think?" I said.

"The more I see him, the less bright he seems. She's a living reminder that not *all* a-holes are Republicans."

"So she doesn't have a career?"

"*He's* her career. She's a non-practicing

lawyer, writes a little, gushy pieces on organic apple farms, stuff like that, they have three young kids, and she's on every board you can name."

"Where do they live?"

"On one of the big old estates south of Kingston — I think it's called River Hill — they bought it about five years ago and did some amazing reno, it's been in magazines. They're definitely working a Kennedy/Clinton/Obama vibe: idealistic hubby, dynamic wife, gorgeous family."

An older woman, distinguished looking, approached and said warmly, "Hello there, Abba."

"Hi, Helen. Helen Newcombe, Janet Petrocelli."

"What a pleasure," she said in an old-money voice. "This food is divine, no surprise. I saw your write-up in the *Times*. So exciting. I hope you're not going to forsake our dear valley now that you're famous."

"Not a chance." Abba turned to me, "Helen's family goes back even before mine. They own half of Kingston."

"Oh, that's ridiculous. We own three-quarters."

"My mom and Helen walked picket lines together back in the early days of the Civil

Rights Movement."

"And we still meet for lunch when Liz comes East. I was distraught when she decamped to Berkeley. Have you met Liz Turner, Janet?"

"I haven't."

"Oh, you have a great treat in store."

Alice Van Wyck appeared, all over Helen Newcombe, "Helen, we're *so* glad you could make it."

"The smartest thing you've ever done, Alice, is hire this woman," Helen said, reaching up and patting Abba on the cheek.

"Isn't she fabulous?" Alice said, without missing a beat. "We consider her the campaign's official chef."

Abba just smiled.

Clark Van Wyck appeared. When he saw me his face fell, but he picked it up pronto.

"Clark, look who's here — Helen Newcombe."

"Your support means an awful lot to me."

Helen Newcombe gestured to the view, "We have a piece of heaven here and we have to save it."

I made a quick decision to plunge in, "Wasn't it terrible about that girl dying up on Platte Clove two weeks ago?"

Both Van Wycks suddenly looked a little gray.

Abba got it instantly and came to my aid, "Yes. And apparently there's some question as to how she died. It may have been murder."

Helen Newcombe perked up — murder always has that effect. She moved a step closer and said, "Oh really? I hadn't heard that. I thought it was an accident, or that perhaps she'd committed suicide."

"Her cellphone has been recovered," I said. "It may contain some evidence."

Alice Van Wyck's left eye twitched. Her husband picked up a bacon-wrapped fig.

"We don't eat pork," his wife snapped.

"It's organic, was humanely raised down in Gardiner," Abba said.

Clark Van Wyck defiantly popped it into his mouth; rage flashed across his wife's face. "It's time for you to give your speech, darling," she said, putting her arm through his and pulling him away.

Helen Newcombe watched them go and then turned to us, "Ambition is not pretty."

Thirty-Seven

It was Saturday morning. Abba's party was that night but I had miles to go before I boogied. I drove up into the Catskills, to Kelly's Farm, and parked right out front. There weren't many cars around, but in a far pasture I did see a naked man with a bit and bridle on, the reins held by a young woman standing behind him, brandishing a whip — she flicked it on his butt and he broke into a smart trot. Tally-ho.

I knocked on the front door. Kelly answered.

"Didn't appreciate the goons," I said.

"They didn't appreciate you."

"I want some answers."

She looked at me for a long moment, then said, "I guess you've earned them."

I followed her into the living room. Some cooking show was on the TV. She switched it off.

"You want a cup of coffee?"

I shook my head. She sat on a couch, I sat on another one.

"Is Clark Van Wyck a regular?"

"Not anymore."

"What happened?"

"He got carried away one night — it was the night of your uninvited visit, actually — and went home with some marks. Attila the Honey saw them. The jig was up."

"Did he tell you that?"

"*She* did. She showed up here last week."

"And she told you it was over."

"She basically freaked out on me — tears, anger, threats. She wanted his whole history. I didn't give it to her."

"She seems like such a natural dominatrix, why doesn't he just get it at home?"

"That same thought occurred to me."

"So did she threaten to shut you down?"

Kelly took a sip of her coffee and smiled slightly. "She may have said something like that. I gave her a little reality check. Clark Van Wyck is a pretty small fish in my pond." She gave me a knowing look. "She got the message."

"Was he a regular with Natasha?"

She nodded. "He sort of fell in love with Natasha. Several of her clients did."

"How long did she work for you?"

"About six months. I liked her from the

git-go. The work didn't seem to bother her. I know it wasn't her dream job but the money is damn good and we're all adults. Nobody was forcing her to show up. But she got more unhappy all the time, like something bad was happening in her life, something that had nothing to do with her work here."

"How could you tell?"

"She was showing up high. Sometimes up, sometimes down. Believe me, I can spot it a mile away."

"Did you ever talk to her about it?"

"I may have asked if there was something she wanted to tell me. But basically that's not my style — I'm the boss, not the mommy. I knew she was saving her money for a move out to LA."

"So you had no idea what was going on in her life?"

"I heard a little talk, from some of my other employees. Her boyfriend came up. She had it for him bad — but he was bad news. Which is the oldest story. When the hell are we women going to learn?"

"Probably sometime around the twelfth of never. Do you think one or both of the Van Wycks killed Natasha?"

She thought for a minute. "I think he's an overgrown kid, basically pretty immature.

She has her eyes on the big leagues. And she'll do *anything* to get there. The other side of that coin is, she's got a lot to lose."

"That's pretty much my thinking." In spite of her siccing Tweedledumb and Tweedledumber on me, I was starting to like this chick. I stood up. "If you hear anything, will you let me know?"

"Maybe."

"Later."

"Drive safe."

Thirty-Eight

I drove back down from the mountains and headed right for the Van Wycks' estate on the Hudson south of Kingston. This stretch of 9W is one big parcel of land after another, a lot of them home to rambling old monasteries and religious retreats. They may not pay taxes, but they preserve the land and that's probably a fair tradeoff. I came to a fancy carved sign reading "River Hill" and turned down the winding drive, the river came into view and on a rise above it sat the house.

Boy, nothing was left to chance at River Hill, no evocative decrepitude here, no neglected tennis court, defunct fountain or spooky leprechauns. Instead it looked like minions popped out and picked up every stray leaf — the lawns were perfect, pond and pool glittered, the flower beds were manicured and regimented, every outbuilding sparkled with a matching coat of white-with-green-trim paint, and there were two red barns. The main house was a huge stately old wooden affair with a portico, a sunroom, and lots of balconies. The Van Wycks were obviously trying to convey old-money assurance, but when I see a place as impeccable as River Hill I read insecurity.

I parked in the circular gravel drive — there were quite a few cars around — got out and knocked on the front door. I heard the sounds of running, screaming children from inside and the door was opened by a fresh-faced young woman in her early twenties, with a young boy hanging off one leg.

"Hi," she said.

"Hi, I was wondering if Alice or Clark were around?"

"Oh gosh, they're somewhere."

The kid started pulling at her leg, "Wanna play, wanna play!"

"Just a second, Dean."

A woman in her thirties wearing an apron and holding a wooden spoon appeared at the far end of the hallway.

"Megan, do you know where the Van Wycks are?"

"I think they're out in the playroom."

The au pair pointed to one of the barns, "Over there."

I headed down the perfectly groomed

paths lined with solar lights and came to the perfect barn with its cow weathervane on top. I knocked on the door. A middle-aged woman appeared.

"Hi, I'm looking for Alice and Clark."

"We're in the middle of a test shot, but come on in."

No cows for this barn, it's original function a distant memory. It had a shiny wood floor, athletic equipment stacked on the shelves that ran along one side, a basketball hoop, and a climbing wall. The place was set up for some kind of filming — in the middle of the floor a gray backdrop hung from a tall metal frame, Clark Van Wyck stood in front of it, a man in a denim workshirt and glasses pushed up on top of his head stood behind a camera aimed at Clark, Alice stood nearby watching with her arms crossed. There were several other people around, including a woman at a make-up table and another manning a small refreshment table. I hung back in the corner by the door. Alice Van Wyck shot me a mildly interested glance, did a double take, and went right back to scrutinizing her husband's efforts in front of the camera.

"That was good, Clark, but try to relax a little more, act like you're talking to an old friend," the director said from behind the camera.

Clark seemed a little uncomfortable — he looked over at his wife and she gave him a tense, encouraging smile. Then he noticed me. He looked taken aback, ran his fingers through his hair, shot his wife a beseeching look.

"Can we take a short break?" she asked rhetorically — when you're cutting the checks you call the breaks.

Clark let out a sigh of relief as the crew headed over to the food table and Alice headed over to me.

"Hi, there," she said with a cold smile. "What can we do for you?"

"I wanted to talk to you and your husband about Natasha Wolfson's death."

"I have no idea who Natasha Wolfson is."

"Let me refresh your memory. She was the dominatrix your husband used to visit, the one he developed an emotional attachment to, who worked up at Kelly's Farm, the farm you visited just last week."

Alice went still, then shot a glance over her shoulder, turned back to me, smiled, and said, "Why don't we take a little walk?"

I shrugged.

"I'll be back shortly, you can proceed without me," she said to the film crew.

I followed her outside and we headed along a path that wound down toward the river. We walked in silence for a moment. The ball was in her court and I waited to see how she was going to play it.

She seemed to will herself to relax, she inhaled deeply through her nose, her shoulders went down, and she turned to me with a warm smile, "We haven't actually been formally introduced. In fact, I don't know your name."

"It's Janet, Janet Petrocelli."

"What a pleasure." She stopped, leaned down and straightened a slightly crooked solar light. Then she touched me lightly on the arm and we continued strolling. "What do you love most about the Hudson Valley, Janet?" she asked, like I was a new friend and we were on our way to tea.

"The people. The land. And the animals, of course."

"You and I have a lot in common. Are you familiar with the work that Rupco does? They build and manage housing for the valley's most vulnerable population — the elderly, the working poor. And of course there's the Clearwater, and Scenic Hudson, which is doing *amazing* things to preserve our landscape. And then there are our two animal sanctuaries. Clark and I are already generous supporters of all of these organizations, but I'd be delighted to make donations in your honor to all five."

"Sorry, I'm not for sale."

She gave me a slight nod and then asked quietly, "What *do* you want?"

"I want the truth."

"You know the truth."

We reached a graceful old boathouse that jutted out into the river. She led us up a flight of steps and along a deck that encircled the second level. We reached the front of the deck — directly across from us, high above the east bank of the river, sat a dignified gray-stone mansion, a living reminder of a lost age, the river rippled in a cool breeze, a sailboat glided past.

"Isn't this glorious?" she said. A few strands of hair blew into her face and she pushed them back. That's when I noticed her hands were trembling.

"I want the *whole* truth."

The muscles around her mouth tensed, I could feel her anxiety rising like a thermometer. "I had nothing to do with that girl's death."

"When did you find out about your husband's visits to Kelly's Farm?"

She closed her eyes tight for a moment. "About a month ago."

"If his relationship with Natasha became public, it would have torn your world apart."

She looked at me and something clicked in her eyes, she had gone from warm to worried and now she turned hard, her jaw clenched. "You think I don't know that?"

"So it was important to you to end it and destroy the evidence."

"*Everything* is important to me. That's just who I am, who I was raised to be. But if you think I'd kill to get my way, you're wrong."

"But you threatened to shut down Kelly's Farm."

"You're goddamn right I did. Do you think it's easy to find out your husband would rather be beaten by a prostitute than make love to you? Especially when he's developing feelings for her. And, yes, I was relieved when I read that she had died. But I didn't kill her."

She looked me right in the eye — and I was pretty damn sure she was telling the truth.

THIRTY-NINE

I was upstairs getting ready to head over to Abba's for her celebratory party. Since there was a chance Chevrona might show up, I was taking a little longer than my usual throw-on-whatever party prep. Zack was definitely going to be there — he and his pal Moose were out on the river and hoped to bring in some fish to get cooked up — so I figured my efforts wouldn't go to waste in any case.

Earlier in the week I'd called Josie and invited her to the party; she'd said the Maldens wouldn't let her out. I decided to make one last try with a text, since that way there was no chance that her foster parents would hear a ring and step into sentry mode. I sat on the edge of my bed and pecked out "Any chance u can make it tonight? I'll drive up and get u."

She got back to me within a minute.

"Nope. In lockdown mode."

I was disappointed and pissed. It felt like Josie was a part of my Sawyerville family and without her the party just wouldn't be the same, I wanted her to share in Abba's success. And I was angry that she was living with a family that was so rigid and unimaginative. The more I thought about it, the more wrong they felt for Josie. That kid deserved better.

A fierce wave of longing passed over me, so strong I lay down. There was something beside Josie going on here, something that had to do with my own mother and me, with my sadness about her abandoning me.

The thing is, I'd loved her, a lot. She had a kind of magic — she could take a rainy day and turn it into a great adventure. "Oh, who needs silly old school today?" And we would sing and dance around the kitchen, down the long hallway of the East Village railroad apartment, into the bedrooms of her half-asleep drugged-over roommates, and then the crayons would come out and we'd draw elephants and space aliens, bake a cake for breakfast and eat half the batter, she was so pretty and had this goofy laugh and she made me feel so special, and so what if she didn't really care if I went to school or had a decent dinner or clean clothes, so what if she always had a new boy around her, a new man . . . who can blame them, the men, she was so fun, so pretty, so warm and lovable, my mom.

Who left.

Who never got in touch again, who didn't care what happened to her little girl.

My bedroom was lonely and quiet, and lying there I wondered what happened to her. Is she dead? If she's alive, where is she? I hope she's still laughing that goofy laugh, still dancing around the kitchen. Does she ever think of me?

Now my thoughts were spinning, spinning forward to that night when I was fifteen and I didn't give a fuck, I wanted to *live,* and I was drunk and the party was wild and we were out on the lawn and I can't even remember the boy's name if I ever even knew it or what he looked like, I remember he smelled like beer and pushed my skirt up and yanked my panties down and that it was fast and it hurt and then he got up and walked away and I lay there on the scruffy lawn with a plastic tricycle beside me and I felt . . . nothing. Then shame and loathing and anger.

Then my period stopped and I knew and my sad aunt didn't give a shit, nobody gave a shit. And I wanted to abort the baby and I wanted to keep the baby and raise the baby and love the baby. But how could I? I didn't know what a mother was, what a mother did. Except make magic and then leave.

I went to a clinic and scheduled an abortion and then I didn't show up, I just couldn't, and I had a baby girl and I named her Anna and I held her and wanted to keep her. But how could I? I had no money, no job, no place to take her. I was alone. And Anna scared me, her naked vulnerability, *it* scared me — motherhood. So I gave her up when she was two days old, I was too scared.

And now, lying on my bed twenty-seven years later, I'm wondering about her, what her name is, where she lives, who she's grown up to be and if she ever wonders about *her* mother. About me.

And what's left? A crazy quilt of sadness, longing, guilt, anger, regret, curiosity, all of it roiling around just out of sight/mind/heart, pushed down by me for twenty-seven years. Demanding now to be heard, dealt with, called up by my feelings for Josie, by my new life in Sawyerville, by middle age, by time.

But not right now, not tonight. I sat up. The process had begun, but tonight was for celebration, for fun, for putting — as best I could — both Natasha's murder and my emotional reckoning on the shelf.

Just for a little while.

Forty

Sputnik walked into the room and gave me a look that said "Are you okay, mama?"

I reached down and scratched his chest, "Yeah, I'm okay."

There was a knock on the back door downstairs. I went down and let George in. He was resplendent in a porkpie hat set at a jaunty angle, a spangly purple shirt, shiny black slacks, and a mammoth gold horseshoe necklace that Kanye West would consider ostentatious.

"Lookin' good," I said.

"So no Josie?"

"Nah, she can't bust loose."

"Maybe somebody should bust her loose."

He followed me back upstairs and sat at the kitchen table while I went into my bedroom and finished dressing.

"Antonio promised to come when he's finished with his work at the track," George called.

Knowing that just about anything I said would set off a round of reproach, I opted for an Antonio-neutral, "This should be fun tonight."

"What's *that* supposed to mean?" George demanded, appearing in the bedroom doorway.

"It's supposed to mean that I'm looking forward to the party."

"You mean you're looking forward to my abject humiliation if Antonio doesn't show."

I zipped my lip and headed downstairs. George followed, "Oh, so now I get the silent treatment?"

I led us out the back door and headed across the street to Chow as George said, "Boy, for a therapist you sure are passive aggressive."

The party was just getting started. Abba had pushed the tables to the sides and filled the place with tea lights, there was an amazing spread along the length of the counter, a small bar was set up, and people of all ages, sizes, and mojos were pouring in, dressed up fine and ready to party the Hudson Valley night away. Pearl was standing behind the counter, her usual dazedness having morphed into what looked to me like full-fledged shock.

Mad John ran over and wrapped himself

around me.

"Jan-Jan!"

George quickly set up his laptop and speakers for D.J. duty and the music started to roll. The dance floor filled up quickly. Mad John was an interesting dancer: he basically leapt ecstatically up and down in place, occasionally bouncing around a bit, sort of like a human pogo stick.

I got a glass of wine and found Abba in the kitchen pulling more food together, nursing her own glass of vino.

"This is going to be one hell of a shindig." I raised my glass. "To you."

We toasted. "It's important to celebrate the good times," she said. "And this town has been very good to me . . . So what's up?"

"What do you mean?"

"You seem distracted."

"I've got a lot on my mind. You know, Natasha Wolfson and all."

"It's the *'and all'* that I want to hear about."

I sat on a stool and clocked the party through the pass-through.

"I can't stop thinking about Josie."

"I know you can't. And I need extra help around here *desperately.* Put your heart and my restaurant together and it equals time to bring that girl home."

"Easy for you to say."

"I'll be here to help you any way I can, and you know that George, in spite of himself, is about as rock solid as a person can be. That man would take a bullet for you. You'd have a lot of support."

I felt something well up inside me, something big and scary and maybe beautiful. The party was growing wilder by the second, people were calling out congratulations to Abba, popping their heads into the kitchen, raving about the food, dropping off presents.

All the action was comforting somehow, but I felt detached, like there was an invisible shield between me and the hubbub, even the music sounded far away, and then I heard her voice echoing across the years — *Come on, baby girl 'o' mine, it's a special day, a magic day, we're going to go out and play . . .* and she took my hand and swung our arms like we were sisters and off we went, out into the streets of the East Village, to Tompkins Square Park where the trees were the fresh green of spring and she waved to everyone and danced around with her arms out and kissed me and hugged me and loved me . . . she *did* love me, didn't she?

"There she is — my daughter, the star!"

I was pulled back into the kitchen by the arrival of a thin, elegant black woman wearing a silk mandarin jacket and matching pants, her gray hair tight on her head, her face — fine and beautiful with Abba's amber-green eyes — broken into a wide grin of pure pride.

"It's my mama!" Abba cried, looking like a little kid.

They kissed and hugged. Then Abba turned to me, "Janet, this is my mom, Liz. Mom, Janet."

Liz Turner took my hands in hers, "What a pleasure."

"Indeed."

Jay-Z and Alicia Keys singing *Empire State of Mind* came on and Liz broke a few moves. "It's always so good to be back home."

"Mom spends most of her time out in Berkeley these days, though she still has her house up in Catskill. How was your flight?"

"It flew."

"Striped bass for everyone," Zack bellowed as he and Moose blew into the kitchen.

"We got the goods, baby!" Moose dumped a barrel of glistening fish into the huge stainless sink. Moose was six-feet-six of pure male id — he and Zack together were a testosterone orgy.

"I hope you know you're cleaning those suckers," Abba said. Their faces fell. "You heard me, get to work."

Zack came over and gave me a kiss, "Hey, babe."

"Hi, Zack," Liz said.

Zack turned to her, took her hand and kissed it, "Now that the queen is here, this is *officially* a party. This is my buddy Moose."

Moose nodded from the sink, where he was already elbow-deep in fish innards.

"I need a smoke," Liz said, "Keep me company, Janet?"

I nodded, she took my hand and led me out to Abba's small back patio. We sat at a round bistro table, she took a joint out of her bag, lit up, took a toke, blew it out, and then sang:

"Puff, the magic Negro."

We laughed and she offered me the joint, I shook my head.

"I never smoke at home," she said. "My current husband disapproves."

"What does he do?"

"He's a retired professor of African-American studies at UC Berkeley. Lovely man, a bit snooty at times, but well-heeled, great sex, and we're both from the loose-leash school of marriage. It works."

She looked up — the night was black and moonless, tossed with stars. "Look at that Hudson Valley sky. And smell that old man river." The slight breeze carried the river up to town, damp and earthy, loss and promise.

"I'm crazy about your daughter," I said.

"Isn't she something? She's always been an independent little cuss."

"Yeah?"

"I raised her that way. Can't stand that clingy nonsense. You have any kids?"

I hesitated. "No. Never really had the urge. The idea of being a mother scares me."

"There's nothing to it."

A bitter little laugh escaped me.

"I took my cues from the animals," Liz said. "They let their young know they're loved, teach them how to hunt and hide and fight and play, and then it's hasta la vista, baby, mama's got her own bag."

My mom taught me to get my own Cheerios, does that count? Half the time the milk was sour, but they tasted fine dry. And she taught me to expect nothing and trust no one, especially your own fucking mother.

But listening to Liz, I knew with urgent finality what I had always suspected — that it could all be different, that motherhood wasn't rocket science, that I didn't need a degree, that I could trust myself, that women had been raising children for thousands of years and it just took a mix of commitment and discipline, kindness and common sense.

"Liz to Janet, come in please?"

"I'm sorry, I've got a lot on my mind."

"Well, hand it over."

This time there was no stopping the wave, and this time I didn't want to stop it. I stood up.

"I'll be back in a little while," I said.

I ran across the street and got in my car, took out my phone and texted Josie.

"I'm coming for you. Pack light."

"Been packed for weeks."

I pulled out of my driveway and headed toward the thruway. And then, for some crazy reason, I turned on the windshield wipers.

Forty-One

I knocked on the Maldens' front door. Doug Malden opened it; his wife, Roberta, stood behind him.

Now that the moment was here, I suddenly felt vulnerable, presumptuous, rude, guilty. "Hi, I'm Janet Petrocelli, a friend of Josie's."

"And what can we do for you?" Doug Malden asked.

Josie appeared on the staircase behind them. Seeing her, my courage returned.

"You can let Josie go with your blessings," I said.

The Maldens looked at me like I had two heads.

"I want to take Josie back to Sawyerville with me. We're going to talk to her caseworker on Monday and petition family court to make the move legal. I know this is very sudden and not really fair to you, but it's just . . . it's just that I feel very strongly that it's best for Josie. And for me."

Doug Malden took this in, stuck his hands in his pants pockets, and stood up straight.

"And exactly what kind of *family* would you be bringing her into?"

"Me. My family. There's me. There's my pets."

"Your *pets?*"

"Yes. Lois, Bub, Sputnik."

"Sputnik?"

"He's a great guy, terrier mix, scruffy, bright enough, he's crazy about Josie."

"Is he now?"

I nodded.

"Well, my goodness. What could be better for a young girl than to be taken out of a nice clean Christian household and thrown in with a single woman and a dog named Sputnik?"

"I have friends, too, there's Abba and George and Mad John and —"

"Mad John?"

"He's a very upstanding little guy."

"This is outrageous."

"I know it is, and I'm sorry I didn't give you any warning but . . . but . . ." I looked over at Josie, she was beaming at me like a mom at her tongue-tied kid, ". . . but Josie is *loved* in Sawyerville, and I'm taking her back, back home."

Josie came down into the hallway. “Mr. and Mrs. Malden, you’ve been good to me and I’m appreciative, but I belong in Sawyerville with Janet.”

“Don’t you tell me where you belong. I’m the adult here. You’re just a girl,” he glanced down at her bum leg, “a girl with problems.”

Josie looked at him for a long moment, turned, ran up the staircase, and was back in a flash with a suitcase, a backpack, and a laptop. Her way forward was blocked by the Maldens. Then Roberta Malden placed a hand on her husband’s forearm and took a step back, “We can’t force her.”

Doug blew out air and muttered, “This is the damnedest thing.” But he followed his wife’s lead and stepped back.

Josie walked past them and out of the house.

As she and I headed down the front walk to my car, two words kept going through my head: *Oh shit.*

Forty-Two

I wish I could say the drive back to Sawyerville was filled with high spirits, giddy chatter, estrogen-fueled bonding. It wasn't. It was filled with doubt and second-thoughts on my part, and a considerate reserve on Josie's. We touched on the mechanics of her starting back up at Sawyerville High, on working with her caseworker to make the new arrangement legal, and just generally dancing around the gorilla in the Camry.

When we got home, Josie carried her stuff upstairs and reclaimed her old room, Sputnik went frigging shortcakes, Bub flew upstairs and got in the action, Cruella De Cat slunk around with her tail swishing, pretending she didn't care. I had a lot of junque in the room and Josie and I lugged some of it down to my workshop. When she was more or less settled in, she sat on the bed and said, "Thank you."

Now that Josie was here my ambivalence

was receding, morphing into something that felt right and doable, and that simple "Thank you" pretty much sealed the deal. This kid was special and I was one lucky chick to have her in my life. In fact, it kind of felt like I had more to gain from the deal than she did. She'd already forced me to open up and be straight with myself, to look my scariest demons right in the face — to admit that little Anna tore a hole in my heart, that my abandonment by my mom was still a chasm of longing and anger — to practice what I'd preached to my clients for all those years, that denial is a dead-end and closure is a myth, that trauma leaves a scar and that scars can be beautiful, badges of kindness and humanity.

"There's a bunch of people across the street who will be very happy to see you," I said.

"Let's go."

Forty-Three

The party was pouring out into the street in front of Chow, folks smoking and laughing. Inside the dance floor was jammed, food was being devoured, flirtations blooming, heated discussions going down, this was one helluva bash. I scanned the room — no sign of Chevrona.

Mad John saw us and let out a cry of joy that could be heard in Cincinnati, then ran across the room and leapt on Josie, wrapping himself around her. Pretty soon George, Zack, and Abba were giving her their own version of the same. All the attention was a little much for her and she retreated to the kitchen with Abba to help her stay on top of things — Abba being a natural-born host, more concerned with her guests' pleasure than her own.

Zack pulled me out onto the dance floor and we boogied for a while. My heart wasn't into it. It had been a big night for me and I could feel emotional exhaustion coming on.

"You okay, babe?" Zack asked.

I nodded. He danced close to me, our bodies touched.

"You did a mitzvah," he said. "And one mitzvah deserves another — let's head over to your place."

"Not tonight, Zack."

"Why not?"

"I've just got too much on my mind, I'm wrung out."

He looked hurt, in an exaggerated sort of way. Then he shrugged. "All right. I get it."

"In fact, I think I'm going to head home."

He put a hand on the back of my neck, it felt warm and comforting and sexy. "I'm proud of you, Janet."

Just when I thought Zack was too glib, too shallow, too *yo-dude* for me, he did something like this. I kissed him, "Thanks, Zack."

"Let me walk you home."

"That's okay, you stay and have a good time."

Once I got out in the night air, I felt better, the wide open sky, the air growing humid, promising some September heat, that thick enfolding Hudson Valley heat that seemed to kick the world into low gear.

Maybe it could slow down my churning wheels.

I got home and realized that I was too wound up to sleep, so I put Sputs on his leash and we headed down toward the town beach on the Esopus Creek.

In spite of Josie and everything else going on in my life, my mind kept going back to Natasha's death. I'd been gathering a lot of information about a lot of people and it was all swirling around in my head. Which was a good thing. In my practice with my clients I liked to listen and listen and then listen some more. As their stories poured out, their personalities and neuroses slowly took shape and little by little the important stuff began to stand out in relief. Then I could see where they were off track, and how I could maybe guide them to a better place. It was a process that couldn't be rushed and any attempt to come to a quick conclusion or solution usually backfired.

Sometimes I thought of it as throwing all the pieces of a puzzle in the air — they drift back down, come together and form themselves into a coherent picture. There was a certain amount of intellect involved, of course, but there was also intuition, gut, maybe even a touch of psychic energy (not that I believe in that crap) — and a sense not only of what is there, but just as importantly, what isn't.

We reached the beach — a small sandy stretch with a swing set and a bathhouse, a little slice of 1950s Americana sitting happily in the twenty-first century — and Sputnik pulled me down to the water's edge. I let all the players dance through my head: Pavel, Octavia and Lavinia Bump, Collier Denton, Graham, Sally and Howard Wolfson, Julia Wolfson, Kelly, Alice and Clark Van Wyck. And poor Natasha, of course. Fighting for her life. I saw her again, on that bright Phoenicia morning: frightened but full of hope, determined to pull herself together, to get away from pills, Pavel, and . . . ? What? Who? I had a gnawing feeling that there was some connection I was missing, some piece I hadn't grasped yet.

I took Sputnik off his leash and he charged into the water. I went and sat on a swing and pushed myself gently back and forth. My mind kept going back to that hothouse nexus down in Stone Ridge — Collier Denton had blackmailed Pavel into supplying Natasha with pills, Denton was capable of nasty deeds, Pavel was amoral, Graham too, Octavia rich and capricious enough to buy a murder. The other players tugging at the corners of my mind were the Wolfsons. Howard Wolfson seemed like a man who wanted to squeeze one more chapter out of his life — with Sally written out. I got a whiff of desperation from Sally, who seemed oddly fragile and frightened behind her veneer of success. And then there was Julia. In rough shape, addicted, *prima facie* evidence of the Wolfson family's pathology.

I took out my cell and called her.

"Hi, Julia, it's Janet Petrocelli."

"Oh hi, how are you?"

"I'm good, and you?"

"Much better than the last time you saw me. I was a hot mess." She laughed in a forced actressy way. "I'm actually in recovery. Five days clean and dry."

"That's great — *bon courage.*"

"Yeah, thanks. I want to do it for Natasha."

"Listen, is there any chance we can get together?"

"Yes, sure, of course. What's this about?"

"I'd just like to talk to you a little more about your sister, and your family."

There was a long pause and I heard her light a cigarette. "Wow, this is really weird that you called."

"How so?"

"Well, you know, I'm working the program, amends and all that." Then she laughed, forced again, mirthless.

"You think you owe me an amend?"

There was another long pause, more smoking. "Well, yes, kind of. I wasn't totally straight with you. About my family, my folks, that stuff. I know more than I let on."

"Do you want me to come down to the city?"

"I'm actually coming upstate on Monday. Can you meet me at Walkway Over the Hudson at around six?"

"Yes. Which side?"

"Highland, on the west side of the river."

"See you there."

Forty-Four

Sputnik shook himself semi-dry, I put his leash back on and we walked up the hill and around the side of my building toward the back door.

"Janet."

I turned to see Chevrona coming toward me.

"Oh, hi there."

She reached me and we stood in a little pool of shadowy light. The party music echoed and throbbed from down the street. She looked crisp and sharp in a white oxford and black slacks that fit *just so.*

"You're not going to the party?" she asked.

"I've been. I didn't know you were coming, I looked for you."

"Long day at work. But I'm here now."

"You are."

She reached down and petted Sputnik.

"That cellphone is destroyed, was in the water too long."

"Damn."

"Yeah."

"It's been a long day for me, too. I brought Josie back down from Troy, she's going to be living with me."

"That's great news. She's such a good kid. A big adjustment for you, though."

"Yeah, it is. But I'm ready. I think."

"If there's ever anything I can do . . . I'm here for Josie. And for you."

There was a long loaded silence. I looked into her eyes and they were filled with that mix of hard and soft that I found so intoxicating. She reached up and rubbed the back of her neck.

"So . . ." she said.

"Yeah . . ."

"I'm getting the feeling you want to knock off for the night."

"Well, yeah, maybe a good idea. I am kinda wrung out."

The strains of Otis Redding singing *Try a Little Tenderness* drifted over from the party.

We looked at each other.

Then she took me in her arms and we started to dance.

FORTY-FIVE

I woke up a little dazed the next morning. After our dance, Chevrona and I had said good night with a kiss — it wasn't a big kiss (it wasn't that small, either) but there was a lot in it and it sent a luscious moist shiver racing up and down my body. What it all meant I wasn't sure, where it was all leading I had no idea. I did know that it felt good and right, but also that it complicated my life at a time when that was the last thing I needed. I made a decision to let it play out slowly; I was pretty sure Chevrona was on the same page.

I lay in bed listening to Josie move around the apartment. There was something comforting about the footfalls, drawers opening, water running, but I also knew that my freedom was suddenly curtailed. No more slothful days where I didn't bother to get dressed or do the dishes, no more PB&Js for dinner, no more dragging Zack upstairs for a quickie, no more being responsible for my own needs and no one else's.

After getting cleaned up and dressed, I walked out to the main room to find Josie sitting at the kitchen table on her laptop.

"Good morning," I said.

"Did you know that the Bump family fortune was made in steak and kidney pies?"

"I'm not surprised, Lavinia Bump seems to live on them."

"They sound kinda gross but they sure are popular. Bump Pies was formed in 1811 and is still the best-selling meat pie in England."

Josie went back to her Internet as I made myself a pot of coffee.

"Now *this* is interesting," she said, eyes glued to the screen.

"What?"

"In 1981, Octavia Bump's betrothed died in a suspicious accident at the Bump estate in Kent, England."

"What happened?"

"Francis Litchfield fell from a third floor balcony and fractured his skull. The only witness was Octavia Bump, who was with him on the balcony."

"Were any charges brought?"

"There was an inquest and the death was ruled accidental. Octavia said that a gust of wind came up and blew her hat off the balcony. Litchfield chivalrously tied to grab it and overreached, tipping himself over the balustrade. But Jane Ormond, another English blueblood, claimed that she and Litchfield were in love and that he had gone to the Bump estate to break off his engagement with Octavia."

I could just picture Octavia, that raging bundle of entitlement, passion, and impulse, shoving Francis Litchfield to his death after he told her he was leaving her. And if she did it to him, what would stop her from pushing Natasha to her death from the Platte Clove so that Pavel would be hers, all hers? She claimed that she was home that night painting, but there were no witnesses. And I wasn't surprised that the inquest had led to nothing — if the British legal system was anything like the American, money talked and the rich walked.

"Pavel better go through with their marriage," I said.

"I'll say."

"Listen, I'd appreciate anything you could find out about Sally and Howard Wolfson. And also Collier Denton."

"I'll nose around," she said, standing up and heading to the fridge. "I made a little pancake batter. It's multigrain with blueberries."

"I don't really eat much breakfast, Josie."

She looked hurt for a moment, but took out the batter, put a pan on the stove, tossed in a little butter, turned on the heat. "I'll just make myself a couple."

I felt a stab of guilt, would it kill me to eat a pancake? But if this new arrangement was going to work I had to have some control, feel like I wasn't giving up all my freedom, everything I'd worked to create in my new upstate life.

"Listen, Josie, I'd like to set a few ground rules for our life together."

"Good idea," she said, spooning the batter into the pan.

"If I seem distracted or involved, just leave me alone. I'd like to keep dinner informal, if either one of us is inspired to cook, fine. If not, it's every gal for herself. I'll buy you a television for your room, please keep the volume low, or better yet get headphones. Zack spends the night once in awhile, I don't want to feel inhibited about that. I'm not your maid — I expect you to clean up after yourself and do your own laundry. I'll give you thirty dollars a week allowance. How does all that sound?"

"It sounds reasonable. Now it's my turn.

If my door is closed, please knock and *wait* for my okay before you come in. I love to cook, so count on me for dinner most nights, if I'm not around check the freezer — I'll mark everything so you won't find any mystery meat. If you and Zack want to screw on that table, go for it, I'll make myself scarce. As for the allowance, Abba hired me last night as sous chef-slash-waitress-slash-whatever, so I'd like to contribute seventy-five dollars a week to general household expenses. How does all that sound?"

We just smiled at each other. Then she turned and flipped the pancakes.

"Any chance I can get that first batch?" I asked.

Forty-Six

It was a sweet September evening in the valley — mild with just a hint of October's nostalgic nip, the trees showing their first dapples of red and orange — but I couldn't really savor it because I was heading down to Highland for my meeting with Julia Wolfson and I was too focused on what she might tell me. I drove through New Paltz and headed east on 299 to 9W, then north a few miles to the western end of the Walkway Over the Hudson.

The Walkway is a former railroad bridge, a cool steel trellis structure that looks like it was built with a giant erector set. When it opened in 1889 it was the first bridge over the Hudson and the longest bridge in the world; today it's the longest pedestrian bridge. It carried trains until 1974 when it was damaged in a fire. A lot of people wanted to tear it down, but some prescient folks saw its potential, and in 1992 efforts began to turn it into a walkway that would link up with trails and bike routes on either side of the river. It opened in 2009 and everyone was hoping for fifty thousand visitors in its first year — it got seven hundred thousand, and has turned into a serious economic engine for the entire valley, especially Poughkeepsie, where it has jolted up the funky 'hood surrounding its eastern end.

I parked in the lot and hoofed down to the entrance area. It was a few minutes after six, twilight was descending and the bridge stretched out in front of me like an invitation. People were pouring across in both directions, a Valley hodgepodge of ages, colors, and classes, dogs and skaters and runners. But there was no sign of Julia and I began to worry that she'd pull a no-show, that she'd gotten cold feet on her promise to level with me.

But then she appeared, "I'm *so* sorry I'm late," she said, too apologetic in that way insecure people are. She looked pretty great, hip and pulled together in black slacks, black silk shirt, and a blazer, eyes clear, skin glowing. But she also seemed fragile and high-strung, and I felt for her — early sobriety is never easy.

We set off across the walkway. "Thanks

for meeting me," I said.

"Do you know why I'm here?"

I shook my head.

She patted her bag. "I have some of Natasha's ashes, I'm going to scatter them off the bridge. It's what she would have wanted. We grew up just down the river, she loved the valley, it was home. One of the last times I saw her, we took this walk. We were both finally starting to put things together, how Sally and Howard had fucked with our heads, how much we had in common, how we could be friends, *should* be friends."

"What do you mean about your folks?"

She reached into her bag and took out a pack of American Spirits and lit up, sucked deep on the smoke, her last drug left. "It was schizo time — in public we were their adored little girls, trotted out at parties and events, talked about on TV, written about. But at home they either ignored us or put us down, but in subtle ways, especially Sally. It would have been better if she'd just slapped us around — at least we would have known where we stood."

"Like what subtle ways?"

"Oh man, where to begin? When I told her I wanted to be an actress, she said, 'But do you *really* have the talent?' And when Natasha brought her first CD home, she cooed over it but then never unwrapped it. She once said to us, 'Thank God you're both pretty, because *serious* careers are out of the question.' By the way, she must be feeling a little guilty — she called and gave me their cell numbers."

"What about your dad?"

"I barely know the guy. I can count on one hand the times we did stuff, just the two of us. And he used to flirt with Natasha, I guess he thought it was cute, but it was *creepy.*"

"Flirt how?"

"He'd admire her figure, tell her she had a lot of sex appeal, play with her hair. For all I know it went further."

"You think he actually molested her?"

"I don't know, Natasha never said he did. But last time I saw her, she talked a lot about what went down between them. She wanted to confront him."

A chill shot through me. "*Did* she confront him?"

"I don't know."

Even if Howard Wolfson didn't molest Natasha, it sounded like he was way out of line and when a girl gets those kind of messages — well, Natasha's sexual history speaks for itself. If actual abuse took place and she did confront him, maybe with threats to go public, could it have driven him to murder her?

"Is that what you wanted to tell me?"

"That's one thing. There are a couple more — Howard isn't Natasha's biological father."

"Whoa."

"Yeah, he adopted her when she was three-and-a-half. Mom had Natasha when she was like nineteen. She was at Sarah Lawrence on a scholarship, studying journalism, she wanted to be Barbara Walters, the *last* thing she wanted was a kid."

"Who is Natasha's father?"

"Some classmate Sally dated a few times. He gave her the money for an abortion but the doctor told her she'd waited too long and it would be risky."

"What happened to him?"

"He moved to Texas, I think, a million years ago, Natasha never met him."

"Natasha told you all this?"

"Yeah. She forced it all out of Sally, only like five years ago." She took a deep drag on her smoke. "Lot of fucking secrets in this family, feels *so* good to get it out. Sally couldn't deal with having a kid, she was obsessed with her career, so she dumped Natasha at her dad's, right over there in Poughkeepsie. She visited maybe once a month."

Another sad new wrinkle to Natasha's story — she was unwanted to begin with, essentially abandoned for the first years of her life.

"So your mom is from Poughkeepsie?"

"Yeah, her dad was a school custodian. Try *prying* that out of her. In her official bio, it says he was an educator." She laughed, sharp and hollow. "I'll give her this — she's worked like a dog to get where she is today. A rabid dog."

"What about your dad?"

"He's from outside Philly. His dad was a pediatrician. My folks are a weird match — Irish Catholic working-class girl meets Jewish doctor's son. Of course, Howard was already half famous when they met. Famous *and* married."

"Your mom broke up the marriage?"

"Oh yeah, she just moved right in for the kill."

Julia was talking rat-a-tat-tat, the words pouring out on a wave of pent-up emotion, and I got the strong sense that she didn't really know who *she* was. Her childhood had been a confusing one, full of conflicting messages, lax discipline, ostensible privilege masking parental disengagement, hostility, and maybe worse. There was no guidance, no help developing a sense of herself — now she was trying to build a life on a foundation of sand.

"How do you know all that?"

"Because I ran into his first wife at a party and she went on a drunken rant." She stopped, dropped her cigarette and ground it out. "Payback's a bitch, Mom." She let out another laugh, this one of bitter triumph. We started walking again.

"You mean your father's cheating?"

"Yeah. And this time I think it's serioso. Guess who's freaking out? Sally's got a great colorist but her roots are showing. I almost feel sorry for her. *Almost.*"

"Strange that they weren't ambitious for you two girls."

"When Natasha's CD made a splash Sally was perturbed, like jealous. Howard barely noticed."

Everything Julia was telling me fit my profile of Howard Wolfson as detached, entitled, and leading with his very-male ego, and of Sally Wolfson as a driven narcissist. But even narcissists often want their children to do well because it confirms their high opinion of themselves and raises their stature in the world. Sally's jealousy of her daughters was puzzling. There was some missing element to my understanding of her psychology.

"Did your mom have a rough childhood?"

"Oh yeah. That's the other thing I wanted to tell you. She *never* talked about it, she's very ashamed, but her own mom was bat-shit."

We'd almost reached the midpoint on the Walkway — below us a tugboat was pulling a barge downriver.

"Your grandmother?"

"Yes, I mean she was really crazy, schizophrenic. When Sally was about five she was institutionalized." She pointed to the east bank, "Right over there, at Hudson River State Hospital."

Hudson River State was notorious in psychiatric circles. A massive gothic complex that first opened in the late nineteenth century, it's original good intentions gradually gave way to warehousing, neglect, and even abuse of its patients, the foreboding red brick buildings a perfect symbol for the horrors within. It was finally closed for good in 2003.

"And when did she die?"

"She killed herself when Sally was fifteen. Like I said, none of this has ever been discussed."

"But you and Natasha talked about it?"

"Oh sure. And we'd ask Sally questions

but she'd always brush us off. She has this weird ability to just shut out things she can't handle. Wish I'd inherited *that.*"

"Does your mom have any relatives still in the area?"

"Her brother, crazy ass Uncle Bob; he still lives in Poughkeepsie. I've only met him once, she keeps him hidden but good. But I'm sick of talking about my mother. She's a stone-cold bitch and I hate her."

She reached into her bag, took out a simple metal box and opened it. It was filled with Natasha's grainy gray remains. She reached her hand in and raked her fingers through the ashes, like she was trying to connect with her sister one last time.

"Thanks for looking out for Natasha," she said.

It meant a lot to me that she said that. "Hey, we're all in this together."

"You know when I was really little, me and Natasha were close, she was my big sister, we'd play hide and seek, watch TV, do each other's hair. But we were sent to different schools, even in grade school, and we never got close again. But in the last few months we were starting to. We were both scared. But we realized that when it came to family, all we had was each other."

She grew very still and her eyes filled with

tears. Then she reached out over the railing and tipped the box — Natasha's remains, picked up by the breeze, billowed through the air and down to the river below.

Forty-Seven

When I got back to my car, I called Josie, "Can you see if you can find me an address for a Robert Cleary in Poughkeepsie?"

"Sure thing. Let me get to the computer . . . here we go, there's a Robert Cleary at 218 Henderson Street."

I punched the address into my map app. "Thanks."

"Listen, Janet's Planet is a little disorganized. How would you feel about me taking an inventory of your stock?"

"Grateful and beholden."

"I'll accept both."

I headed over the Mid-Hudson Bridge and into Poughkeepsie. Po'town is the biggest city in the mid-Hudson area, and it's a pretty interesting place, struggling but with lots of cool architecture, a multi-everything population, home to Vassar and its bucolic campus. Like a lot of the valley, you feel it has turned a corner and its worst days are behind it.

Henderson Street was just outside of downtown in a semi-rundown neighborhood of small single-family houses. Robert Cleary's house was only partially visible because the front yard and driveway were piled with mounds of *stuff* — rotting furniture, cardboard boxes filled with who-knows-what, old appliances; some of the mounds were covered with orange or blue tarps, others just sat there moldering. The house itself had gutters hanging loose, torn window screens, bent siding. I made my way up to the front door and knocked. No answer. I knocked again. Then again.

Finally a man's voice called, "Go away!"

"Can I talk to you a minute?"

"Get your ass off my property!"

"I want to talk to you about your mom, Rose Cleary."

Silence.

Then, in a much smaller voice, "What about her?"

"I'm just interested in her, in what she was like."

More silence, then the sounds of about a dozen locks being opened, finally the door opened a crack — a sickening moldy smell poured out. Then a sliver of face, one half-mad eye that looked at me with great wary curiosity.

"You from social services?"

"No, I'm not."

The sliver of face pressed closer to the crack, the eye looked me up and down.

"Who're you?"

"My name is Janet, I'm a friend of your niece, Natasha. She was murdered."

"Hope they got her mother, too."

"I want to talk about *your* mother."

Something softened in the eye. "She's dead."

"I know she is. And I know she had a hard life."

"You got that right. Wasn't fair."

"I know it wasn't. It was sad. Sad for her and sad for you."

The eyeball looked me right in the eye, a challenge. I met the look.

The door opened halfway. Bob Cleary looked like he could be anywhere from forty to ninety, as skinny as a cadaver, all bones and angles, the palest skin, enormous cheekbones jutting out, full head of dirty — *really* dirty — blonde hair.

He scrutinized me one last time, then opened the door all the way, turned and walked down the hallway — correction, the tiny path that wound through the detritus that was piled almost to the ceiling. Out of the corner of my eye I caught sight of a mouse running over the debris, then another. The smell was almost overpowering — animal excrement and mold and rotting food and I'll stop there.

I followed Bob down the pathway and into a room near the back of the house. Again, stuff was piled almost to the ceiling — newspapers, clothes, plastic bags filled with who-knows-what, old lamps and clocks and appliances. There was one tiny circle that was semi-clear, it held a recliner, a TV — Bob was watching QVC on mute — a microwave and a half-fridge.

Bob Cleary wasn't the first hoarder I'd met, and the condition definitely has varying degrees of severity (on a scale of 1–10, I'd peg Cleary at 11).

Although the room looked like an undifferentiated mass of junk to me, Bob — in classic hoarder behavior — went right to one of the piles, rummaged around for just a second and then pulled out a photo album. He looked down at it for a moment, intently, ran his hand over it, sort of reverentially, then he handed it to me. Cutout letters across the front read MOMMY.

He sat down in the recliner and watched me. I leafed through the album — there were black-and-white shots of Rose Cleary as a little girl, a pretty girl with a bright smile, dressed for church, playing at a lake, posing outside her house with her parents. I'd seen a thousand pictures just like these during my career as a collector — hopeful records of hopeful moments, I found them evocative and touching.

Rose was a teenager in the later shots — which had that unmistakable 1950s look — laughing with friends, working behind a soda-fountain, on the arms of a young man I assumed was her husband-to-be, but there was a hint of wildness in her eyes, of the madness that would later claim her. There were wedding pictures, heartbreaking shots of Rose in a long white dress that she looked uncomfortable in. In one shot she was looking off to the side, distracted, troubled — had she begun to hear voices, to hallucinate, was she hiding a terrible secret from her groom, from the world, from herself?

Then came the Sears-Roebuck shots of Rose with little Sally and Robert. Sally was a few years older and was already filled with determination, looking straight into the camera. Robert seemed a little dazed, and Rose is starting to look crazy, her mouth twisted slightly and covered in too much red lipstick.

There were only a few more pictures and

they were obviously taken on the grounds of Hudson River State. In them she's wearing a thin housedress and is either smiling like a madwoman — manic, teeth bared — or looking dazed and heavily medicated, barely there. In one shot she just looked like the saddest person in the world, a woman who knew that she was sick beyond repair and had lost her children, her life. In these last shots, little Robert is protective of his mother, either hugging her leg or standing in front of her, tall, chest out. Sally, on the other hand, stands away from her mother, embarrassed and angry.

I closed the album and when I looked up, Bob Cleary was crying.

I had found what I was looking for and there really wasn't much more to say.

"Thank you for showing me this."

"Can you give me some money?"

I handed him forty dollars and left.

Forty-Eight

I headed back across the river, trying to piece it all together. It was impossible not to feel for the poor guy. And for all the Wolfsons — the father, Sally, Julia, Natasha. And, of course, for the original victim: Rose Cleary. Struck down by a terrible, incurable disease. The legacy of her madness was still being played out.

Sally spent her childhood in the shadow of her mother's schizophrenia and that helped me understand the root of her narcissism. How painful and confusing and enraging it must have been for her to watch Rose manifest the bizarre early symptoms of the disease, be institutionalized, slowly degenerate, and then die a terrifying and lonely death. Sally was just a kid trying to make sense of the world, and when a child isn't receiving the love and attention she needs from her parents, she'll often turn inward for that love, create a private Idaho where all the attention is on her, where she *is* loved and valued. My hunch was that little Sally Cleary did just that.

And although grown-up Sally may have wanted children for a lot of intellectual and social reasons — to solidify her marriage, meet the world's expectations, prove how capable she was — my guess was that she was completely unprepared emotionally to surrender the spotlight to her new co-stars, to nurture them, to see Natasha and Julia as anything but extensions of herself. And, critically, to be deeply envious of her daughters. They, after all, had the affluent and seemingly secure childhood that she was denied. And — as children will — they took their own privilege for granted, with no understanding of their mom's suffering.

There are a lot of myths about motherhood, chief among them that all women have the maternal instinct. The truth is that a fair number of mothers are ambivalent, and a small percentage actively hate their child pretty much from day one. Suddenly there's a new and completely dependent life in her arms. Goodbye, freedom; hello, responsibility. Then there's money — forget that Xmas trip to Cabo. And hubby is cooing over the kid and may be less interested in sex, at least with *mom.* Of course, the world now defines her just that way — as *a mother.* The kid sucks up all the attention — for a lot of women this can be unbearable, engendering envy and even rage.

Since motherhood is supposedly sacred, women feel guilty about these feelings and they play out in passive-aggressive ways. Sally never opening Natasha's CD is a classic example. A lot of my most f'ed up clients had mothers who should never have taken on the job.

I headed east toward New Paltz. There was one more stop I wanted to make. I had this gnawing feeling that I was missing some vital connection in the puzzle, and that Pavel and Denton were the missing links.

I headed up over the Shawangunks as night descended over the valley. I drove past Mohonk Mountain House and down through the hip little hamlet of High Falls, home to offbeat restaurants, reclusive movie stars, and one mother of a waterfall. I continued on into Stone Ridge and parked in town near the start of Leggett Road. I sat for a moment gathering myself, then I grabbed a small flashlight and set off. Bumpland was about a mile down the road, and I tried to look like an ordinary soul out for a little nighttime hoof as I hustled in that direction.

I reached the western edge of the estate, where its stone walls began. I hopped over the wall and set off across the expansive, tree-dotted lawns toward the garage. The gnomes and elves that dotted the lawns were hardly a reassuring sight, in the darkness they all seemed to be moving toward me — like I was in a horror movie and they were going to tear me to shreds before gleefully devouring my internal organs.

I approached the garage. There were no lights on in Pavel's apartment. Looking past it, I saw the glowing main house with a bunch of cars parked in front — maybe Lauren Parker-Lipschitz was over there finalizing the *joie.*

I reached the garage and ducked inside. It was dark but I could make out the hulking shape of the Bentley and the Rolls. I headed for the stairs at the back and went up. The door was unlocked and I went in. There was a little bit of ambient light pouring in the windows and I waited while my eyes adjusted. Slowly things came into focus. The place looked even sparser than before, lonely, abandoned, as if no one spent time here anymore. And why should Pavel hang in these humble quarters, now that he was weeks away from being lord of Bumpland, loaded to the gills? Although judging by

Octavia's amorous appetites he was going to be *earning* that dough.

I went into the kitchen and started to open drawers and cupboards and shine the flashlight on the contents. It was all pretty barebones. I went into a nearby closet — nothing but broom, mop, trash bags. I slowly worked my way around the whole room, trying not to miss any potential hiding place. Cards, chewing gum, cigarettes, maps, a few books, old copies of *Details, Maxim,* and *Men's Health,* a lot of dust, not much else. I went into the bathroom, just a few half-empty shampoo bottles and slivers of soap, no toothbrush even, the medicine chest had a bottle of Advil, a roll of dental floss, a pack of razors. I rummaged around under the mattress, then opened the closet. Most of the clothes were gone, there were a couple of pairs of shoes on the floor. I reached my hand inside them, nothing. I checked the pockets on the shirts, slipped my hand into the pocket of a leather windbreaker — and felt a prescription bottle. I took it out and shined the flashlight on the label.

The drug was oxycodone. The patient was Collier Denton. The prescribing doctor was Howard Wolfson.

Forty-Nine

I pocketed the bottle and got the hell out of there as stealthily as I could, dashed across the grounds, and made my way up Leggett Road to my car. Driving back to Sawyer-ville, I felt strangely exhilarated: this was the missing link I was looking for. Howard Wolfson had supplied Pavel with the drugs that he had used to get Natasha hooked and send her into the downward spiral that ended in her death. But the prescription had been written to Collier Denton — how did Denton connect to Howard Wolfson? I needed to have a little one-on-one with Wolfson. Soon.

When I got home, Josie had a late dinner waiting — an amazing lasagna, Italian bread, and a salad. It felt pretty damn cozy to walk upstairs and smell garlic and herbs, to sit down to one of my favorite meals.

"This is dee-licious," I said.

"Thanks."

"Did you make it over to Sawyerville High today?"

"I did. We came to a mutual agreement that I would start in the spring semester."

"A *mutual* agreement?"

"Yes. I had my school in Troy e-mail them my transcript and they agreed to my plan. I want to use the fall to get up to speed at Chow, and get Janet's Planet inventoried — and up on the web, if you'll let me."

"Hey, fine with me. And did you make that appointment to see the orthopedist?"

"I did, yes. Thank you."

I filled Josie in on the latest developments. "I'd appreciate any information you could find on Howard Wolfson."

After dinner, Josie went over to Chow, I did the dishes and then called Julia Wolfson and got her dad's cell number, which I called.

"This is Howard."

"Hi, this is Janet Petrocelli, the friend of your daughter Natasha. We met at her memorial."

"What can I do for you?"

"I'd like ten minutes of your time."

"I can give you five right now."

"Actually I'd rather meet in person, if that's at all possible."

"Can you give me any idea of what this is about?"

"Did your wife tell you I think Natasha was murdered?"

There was a pause. When he spoke again, his voice was softer. "She mentioned something. I appreciate your concern for Natasha, but she was a troubled girl. I think she committed suicide."

"That's what I'd like to discuss with you. Just a few minutes of your time. That's all I'm asking for. I'll be happy to drive down to you."

There was another pause.

"My wife is in Los Angeles, researching our book on Natasha; a lot of her friends live out there. She'll be back the day after tomorrow."

"It's you that I want to talk to."

He exhaled with a sigh.

"Where are you?" he asked.

"Up in Sawyerville."

"I'm actually having dinner with a friend in Elka Park tomorrow night."

"That's just a few miles from where Natasha died. Have you seen the spot?"

There was a short pause. "I haven't. Sally and I are planning on paying a visit — we may end the book there. It's going to be very tough for my wife, so maybe seeing it myself first is a good idea."

"Why don't I meet you in Elka Park and drive you to the trail. Then I'll bring you back. The whole thing shouldn't take more than twenty minutes."

"All right. Let's do that."

FIFTY

In the late nineteenth century, before cars were invented and travel became a breeze, a lot of fancy families in cities like New York, Philadelphia, and Boston packed up — servants and all — and went away for the whole summer. They liked to build rambling old summer places near each other so they'd have folks of their own class to hang out with. In the Catskills there are several "parks" that date from that era, enclaves created when groups of like-minded families got together and bought big chunks of land, then each took a piece and built a "cottage" on it.

Elka Park is a lot of huge old clapboard houses next to each other in the middle of nowhere. I always get a kick out of driving through it, the history is palpable and the houses are pretty wowing — massive porches, turrets and gables and dormers. Twenty-five years ago you could pick one up for a song, nowadays they're pretty expensive. It didn't surprise me that Howard Wolfson would have a friend there — Elka Park is emblematic of the new Catskills chic.

The next evening I headed up the Platte Clove Road, past the trail head that led to the spot where Natasha was murdered, and on the few miles to Elka Park. I found the house where Howard Wolfson asked me to meet him, it was an immense Queen Anne in such groomed and immaculate condition that it looked like it had been airlifted in from Disney World. I parked and knocked on the door. An attractive youthful woman I pegged as somewhere in her botoxed late thirties answered and gave me a big showbiz smile, I thought I vaguely recognized her, maybe from one of those determinedly upbeat daytime television shows that all blend together into a cozy/creepy blur.

"You must be Janet," she said, her delivery a little sly, a touch of irony slipping out from behind the perky mask.

"I am, yes."

She didn't introduce herself, so maybe she was some kind of semi-celeb and she assumed I recognized her.

Or maybe she was just a bitch.

She took a step out onto the front porch

and looked around in an exaggerated way. "You haven't seen a stalker around, have you? Blonde, a little jowly, driving a silver Mercedes?" I shook my head. "Oh, that's right, she's out in LA, being ghoulish. Type casting." She stepped back into the house and called, "Howard, that woman is here."

I was leaning toward bitch.

Howard Wolfson appeared. He looked a lot more relaxed than he had at the memorial. In fact he looked rested, handsome, and a little studly in a blue denim workshirt and khakis.

"Hurry back, darling," the woman said, putting a hand on his chest in a proprietary way and giving him a little kiss.

The other woman — younger and more attractive than Sally — but not a bimbo, which in some ways must be making it even harder. A bimbo can be dismissed as a man thinking with his dick. With a peer, things get more complicated. And poor Sally, her jealousy had driven her to stalk her rival — although from the looks of things the contest was over and a winner had been declared.

Just as we set off for Platte Clove, my cell rang. It was Josie.

"Hi, honey, is everything okay?"

"I just discovered something on the Internet that I think you'll find *very* interesting," she said.

"I can't wait to hear it, but this isn't a good time. I'll be back in about an hour."

We drove in silence for a few minutes and then Howard said, "This isn't going to be easy for me."

"How are you doing with it all?"

"I've learned something from Natasha's death. Which is just how truly selfish I am. I was a lousy parent. Being a dad didn't really interest me much. Natasha paid a price for that."

"Julia told me you adopted her."

He looked over at me. "She did, did she?"

"Yes, and that you were overly affectionate with her."

He laughed, incredulous. "That's ridiculous. I didn't have much time for Julia, so she imagined I was lavishing all my attention on Natasha and she was jealous. Natasha was an adorable kid. But overly affectionate? No way."

"Apparently Natasha felt you were. That's what she told Julia."

He exhaled in exasperation, "Oh Christ! Like I need this. Believe me, I'm no saint but nothing happened. You know, kids conflate things. I'm really sorry Natasha felt that way. This all adds up to more guilt for me. And, as you may have realized, other aspects of my life are somewhat complicated these days."

I knew he was right that sometimes children, when they grow older, look back at innocent adult affection and sexualize it. It's a tricky, complicated gray area but Howard's response made me think he was telling the truth.

"How's the book coming?" I asked.

His demeanor changed, a faux-grave expression came over him, he clasped his hands together in his lap, and his voice grew emotional and Bill Clintony. "It's coming well, thank you for asking. We're working on the take-away; we want to help our readers move past the traumas in their own lives. And visiting the place where Natasha died will help me with the closure I need. Nothing will bring her back. I know she would want me to move on, to put this tragedy behind me."

Did he really believe that pabulum? It was like he went from real to superficial a-hole in the blink of an eye. In either mode, it was clear that his daughter's death was first and foremost a career opportunity.

We reached the trailhead parking area, which was empty. We got out of the car. It was quiet, except for the wind rustling the tops of the trees, and the air was chill in the rock-cleaved clove, this untamed landscape, capable of claiming a human life in the blink of an eye.

I led Howard down the trail; we could hear the rushing water but couldn't see it yet. The path wound down and around an increasingly steep slope, the ground was covered with pine needles and it was easy to see how someone could slip and then start to slide and be unable to stop themselves, their downward momentum growing with each inch, until they reached the edge and went over. I didn't like this place.

We reached the spot where Natasha spent her last moments alive. From here you could look down into the gorge and see the rushing torrent, the waterfall, and the pool surrounded by large rocks. I gripped a nearby tree.

"This is it," I said.

Howard stood there, lost in thought. It was hard to read the expression on his face, then he surprised me with a heartfelt, almost inaudible, "Poor Natasha."

We stood in silence for what seemed like a long time. Then we turned and headed back up the trail.

"You know she was on a lot of drugs those last months," I said as we walked.

"I suspected as much. Do you think it was

heroin?"

"I know what it was, and so do you."

"What do you mean?"

"She was on oxycodone, Vicodin, Adderall, and a few others."

"Where was she getting them?"

"From you."

"What are you talking about?"

"Howard, I've got proof."

"Proof of what? What the hell are you talking about?"

I pulled out the oxycodone bottle and handed it to him. He studied it.

"I didn't prescribe this. Who the hell is Collier Denton?"

"Don't play cute with me."

"Don't *you* play cute with *me*."

"You expect me to believe you didn't write this scrip?"

"You're goddamn right I do. If this is your idea of a joke, it's not funny. Were you put up to this by that crazy wife of mine? Bringing me down here and then springing this on me."

He pulled out his iPhone and ran his finger over it. "This scrip was written on May 11th. I was traveling from May 8th to the 14th." He held the phone out to me, "Here's my calendar. I was in San Antonio, Phoenix, and Seattle."

I didn't have to look at the evidence. I knew this guy was telling the truth.

Fifty-One

I delivered Howard back to his mistress and headed down to Sawyerville, eager to find out what Josie had discovered. Things were coming together quickly — Sally Wolfson had to have been the source of the pills that greased her daughter's slide — but there was still one unanswered question: what was the connection between Sally Wolfson and Collier Denton?

When I got back to Sawyerville, I headed over to Abba's. I was exhausted but energized and ravenously hungry. The place was pretty crowded and I saw Abba and Josie hard at work in the kitchen so I sat at the counter, out of their hair. Pearl shambled over.

"I'll have the special," I said, nodding toward the daily chalkboard — Fish Tacos.

Pearl brought her pencil to her lips, moistened it and began to write.

"How do you like the new addition?" I

asked, indicating Josie.

Pearl looked up at me and a smile slowly spread across her face.

Josie's face appeared in the pass-through, "Order up, Pearl. Hey, Janet, I'll be out in a minute." Pearl actually stepped almost-lively as she went to pick up the plates. The times they are a-changin'.

Josie came out from the kitchen and sat on the stool next to mine. She was carrying her laptop, which she opened and put in front of me.

"Look at this," she said, indicating the screen. "It's an interview with Collier Denton that was in *Variety.* The dateline on the article is April 11, 1979, which is the same day that Ian Stock's house burned down."

I scanned the interview; the angle was the plight of the understudy. Denton was understudying Frank Langella in *Dracula* and it was his fourth Broadway understudy gig. The reporter noted that Denton arrived late for the interview but was full of nervous energy, even exuberant. Then I saw the byline: Sally Cleary.

I pulled out my cell and called Chevrona Williams to tell her I'd pick her up at her barracks tomorrow at five for the drive down to Cold Spring.

I signed off with, "Bring handcuffs."

Fifty-Two

"So what's all this about?" Chevrona asked as we sped down the thruway.

I ran her through the whole scenario. She listened thoughtfully.

"I'm not saying it didn't go down that way. But the only piece of evidence you have is one prescription bottle. The rest is circumstantial. Those e-mails are powerful evidence for the defense. And Sally Wolfson is pretty damn sympathetic, not to mention being the victim's mother. I just don't see the DA taking this case."

"You're the one who said we need a confession."

"And you really think you can get one?"

"I'm going to try my best."

I'd given some thought to my timing. Sally had arrived home from her trip to LA in the early afternoon. She'd be tired and want to relax, hopefully with a cocktail, but she'd also be unsettled because she isn't sure what her husband has been up to while she's been away. All in all, in a vulnerable place. And I had a big fat bluff planned.

We arrived at the Wolfsons' house and parked. A middle-aged housekeeper opened the front door.

"Hi, we're here to see Sally, she's expecting us," I lied casually.

The woman smiled and ushered us in.

We walked into the living room to find the Wolfsons sitting on separate couches; sitting on a chair was a thin middle-aged woman in a black dress, her black hair in a chic angular cut; she radiated intelligence and purpose, held a yellow legal pad. It didn't look like a social visit.

Both Howard and Sally stood up when they saw us, their faces registering varying levels of surprise, annoyance, and trepidation.

"I'm sorry to interrupt, but this is important," I said. "This is Detective Chevrona Williams of the New York State police."

No one said anything and the chic woman looked from one Wolfson to the other. Finally Howard walked over to us and said, "This isn't the best time."

"It may not be the best time, but it's *the* time," I said. I walked over to the chic woman and extended my hand, "Hi, I'm

Janet Petrocelli, a friend of Natasha Wolfson."

She looked at my outstretched hand for a moment and then shook it, "Enid Pearlman, I'm Howard and Sally's editor."

"On *Lost Child*?" I asked.

"Yes. It's brilliant. We're planning an enormous push. They're already booked on *60 Minutes* and *The View.*"

"You may want to rethink that."

Sally gathered herself and said, "This is all very fascinating I'm sure, but we're in the middle of an editorial meeting."

"I'm here to talk about Natasha, I have some important information about her death. I think all three of you will be interested in hearing it."

"Well, I certainly am," Enid Pearlman said. She turned to the Wolfsons, "It may be germane to the book."

Howard seemed to resign himself and sat back down; Sally remained standing. I looked right at her.

"Life hasn't been easy for you, has it, Sally?" I turned to Enid. "Did you know that Sally's mother was diagnosed with schizophrenia when Sally was five? Sally's childhood was spent watching her mother get sicker and sicker and finally commit suicide when Sally was fifteen."

"I had no idea," Enid said, looking sympathetically at Sally.

"Imagine how sad and terrifying that must have been? A young girl loves her mother, and needs her mother to love her back. And Sally's mom was lost in a fog of madness and thorazine; their home life was chaos, Sally was teased at school. What child wouldn't be ashamed and angry to have a crazy mother?" I took a step toward Sally. "I'm sorry you had to go through that."

The room was very quiet. Sally's mouth was open.

"You got out of that house as fast as you could, your terrific grades got you a scholarship at Sarah Lawrence. You erased your family, erased the grief and pain. But then you got pregnant with Natasha. Her birth was traumatic, wasn't it? You were angry with yourself for waiting too long to abort her, and angry with her for being born. When you looked at her all you saw was the end of your freedom and dreams. But you were tough and smart and, boy, were you determined. You parked Natasha with your dad and you soldiered on. You got your journalism degree, had a few jobs, but there was very little money and an ambitious girl needs money, money for nice clothes, good haircuts, good restaurants, entrée to places where you meet nice people, nice men. And so you got some money. It took a little blackmail, but what the hell. And then you met Howard, and he was wealthy and successful, and you married him. Then you wrote your first book together and you became famous. Howard adopted Natasha and then you had Julia."

Sally marshaled herself, ran her fingers through her hair, gave me a slightly bemused, pitying look, trying hard to gain control of the situation. "This is *not* germane to the book. It's old history and I think we've heard quite enough of it." She began to move toward me.

Chevrona stopped her with, "Let's just let Janet finish."

"You gave your daughters a privileged childhood and you went through the motions of being a mother, but it never felt real because underneath you just didn't love them. In fact you were bitterly jealous of them — jealous of their privilege and jealous because they were *young.* Their future was your past. And so you undermined them, nothing they did was ever good enough. But they were pretty and they were talented and you *hated* them for it. In fact, when we get right down to it, you hated Natasha from the day she was born."

The room was absolutely still.

"Mini crabcakes?" We all turned to see the housekeeper standing in the doorway holding a tray. The vibe hit her, her face fell and she added in a small hopeful voice, "With my horseradish sauce?"

"Not now, Janice," Howard said *sotto voce.*

Janice retreated.

Sally used the interruption to try to regain her equilibrium. "Your amateur psychologizing is fascinating but alas all wrong. I didn't hate Natasha, I loved her, she was my child, my baby," she said.

"One of your early assignments as a journalist has played an important part in your life, hasn't it, Sally? Do you remember? Sunday, April 11, 1979? You were twenty-one years old and living hand-to-mouth when you got that assignment from *Variety* to interview the actor Collier Denton. He seemed manic and you saw his burn and then you heard about the fire that had killed Ian Stock and you put two and two together and it added up to an opportunity for little Sally Cleary to move one step closer to the golden ring. So you cased Stock's house and you found the evidence you needed and you blackmailed Collier Denton, demanded money, and you've continued to blackmail him ever since. Last spring, after forging your husband's signature on the scrips, you blackmailed Denton to get those pills to Natasha because your marriage was coming apart and your career was on the downswing and you saw a hit book as a way to get your husband back and the limelight back, and the one thing standing in your way was Natasha. You can't have a lost child if she's found herself."

"No!" Sally cried, "The pills were to *help* her. She needed help, she was in trouble. I tried so hard to help her, I sent her e-mails, I called her, I told her again and again how much I loved her."

"I've read those e-mails and underneath the pabulum and bromides, they were undermining, filled with passive aggression. As for the drugs, you knew about her history of abuse, you knew she couldn't handle drugs. But you wanted her dead, you *needed* her dead."

Sally's breathing had grown shallow and a look of panic had taken hold. "This is bullshit, fucking bullshit, you get out of my house!"

"And you knew your husband's latest affair had grown serious and it was driving you around the bend. So you started stalking the other woman's house up in Elka

Park and two weeks ago it all came to a head, you were at the end of your rope, driving around Elka Park like a crazy woman, like your mother! And so you called Natasha and asked her to drive up and meet you —"

"Because I wanted to *help* her!"

"You may actually have deluded yourself into believing that. And you suggested a walk, a nature walk, down that trail, that trail above the waterfall —"

"And she started to argue with me, to accuse me of things, terrible things."

"True things. She told you *the truth.* And so you pushed her."

Sally looked around wildly, a trapped animal, and then she began to race around the room, almost like she was looking for places to hide, clenching and unclenching her fists, then she ran over to a long shelf that held a vase, sculptures, framed photos, and raked her arm across it, sending everything flying, crashing, shattering. Then she turned back to us and looked from person to person — I saw madness in her eyes, the abyss and she was falling — and she started to sob and slowly crumpled to the floor, her face melting and blubbery, her body heaving, wracked.

It was hard to watch but I couldn't stop

now, I needed her to say the words. She had to pay for what she did, that's the deal.

I walked over and stood above her.

"You killed Natasha, didn't you?"

"I wanted to help her, I just wanted to help her, but she yelled at me, she was mean to me."

Like the sick narcissist she was, even now she saw *herself* as the victim. Whatever tinge of sympathy I'd felt evaporated.

"You killed her, say it!"

She looked up at me and bared her teeth and growled, "Yes, I fucking killed her, I pushed her and watched her fall and her head smashed into the rocks and I felt *nothing!* Nothing but *triumph!*"

Chevrona pulled out her handcuffs.

Fifty-Three

Chevrona called for a police car to transport Sally to jail for booking. While we waited for it to arrive, Sally sat like a zombie on one of the sofas. Howard stood behind her, a hand on her shoulder, cold comfort. In the few minutes after her confession he seemed in shock, putting it all together, grasping the magnitude of what his wife had done, but then, subtly, I could see his wheels start to turn. This changed everything for him — and not necessarily in a bad way. Enid Pearlman waited quietly — Chevrona had told her she would need to give a statement — but under her classy and respectful mien, you could tell that she was excited, even electrified by the drama — few things rivet us like another person's fall, add madness and murder to the mix and you have a most seductive stew.

Janice, the housekeeper, had heard the commotion when Sally cleared the shelf, had come out and witnessed her meltdown. She didn't seem to know what to do with herself so she'd brought out the crabcakes, which sat untouched on the coffee table.

I was exhausted and sat on a chair in the corner of the room. After Sally's confession I felt a momentary exhilaration, followed by a hollow feeling, I had done my job, but there was no joy in bringing her down. But there was a lesson. Sally was a victim, of course, a victim of her mother's schizophrenia. It's hard to grasp how painful her childhood must have been. But instead of getting the help she needed and going through a long and wrenching grieving process, she repressed her feelings, shut them down, pretended that she could just "move on" and leave it all behind. So the grief roiled around in her subconscious, but grief will not be denied, it will turn into envy and rage, assert itself in ugly ways. Shakespeare said it like this:

Give sorrow words: the grief that does not speak

Whispers the o'er-fraught heart, and bids it break.

Sally's heart broke and turned her into a monster, a mother capable of murdering her own child.

Several police officers and another detective arrived and took our preliminary statements.

I walked out to my car and stood in the fresh air for a moment. It was dark and the Hudson loomed below, a shimmering liquid ribbon, with the Highlands rising up from the far shore. The night sky was wide and starry and a shiver of hope coursed through me — Natasha's killer would pay for her crime, Josie was waiting at home.

Chevrona and the other detective led Sally to the police car and helped her into the back seat. Chevrona walked over to me.

"You did an amazing job," she said. "What evidence did Sally find that she used to blackmail Denton?"

"You'll have to ask one of them."

"Remind me never to play poker with you."

We were silent for a minute.

Chevrona looked up at the sky. "It's a nice night, a good night."

"It is, it's a good night." I felt my throat tighten. "I'm glad we went through this together."

Chevrona nodded. "I guess we're building a little history."

"I guess we are."

The waves flowing between us were filled with something that felt vast and beautiful.

Chevrona looked down, rubbed the back of her neck. Then she looked up at me.
"You drive safely now," she said.

Fifty-Four

"I'll have the shepherd's pie," Zack said to Pearl, who seemed marginally more *compos mentis* lately.

"I'll take the salmon," I said.

"Cocoa-puffs omelet, *por favor,*" Mad John said. Pearl's mouth fell open at the request and for a moment I wondered if she was having a mini-stroke. Mad John leapt off his chair and started his jumping up and down in place thing, chanting: "I love Pearly, she's my girly!" Then he gave her bohunkus a hearty pinch. Pearl's eyes blinked rapidly, which was reassuring, and then she actually smiled a little and rolled her eyes demurely like a silent-film ingenue. So Pearl was sweet on Mad John. Hey, they made a nice couple.

George walked into Chow, all the riding clothes and accoutrements gone, replaced by solid black. He walked right past us and schlumphed onto a stool at the counter.

"Hey, Georgie, come join us for dinner," Zack called.

George didn't turn to look at us, just stared straight ahead and intoned, "I'm sorry, I am no longer interacting with members of the human race. Why should I? All they do is crush me in return."

"Oh, come on, man, Abba and Josie have collaborated on this amazing shepherd's pie, it has a layer of caramelized onions. And Janet is treating."

George spun around, "Do you really think you can soothe my broken shattered heart with *caramelized onions?* Do you have any concept how deep my despair is?" He got up and shuffled over to us.

"So I take it Antonio left you?" I said.

"You *take it* Antonio left me? You *TAKE IT* Antonio left me!?! The man to whom I gave my heart, my soul, and twelve-hundred dollars in riding-instruction fees has gone back to Argentina, and you glibly 'take it Antonio left me.' You're supposed to be my friend, Janet, but every time my dreams are lying wounded on the sidewalk, you come along and stomp them into oblivion."

"I'm sorry, kiddo."

"I'd kill myself if I wasn't already dead." He grabbed my wineglass and downed the contents. "Pearl, I'd like the watercress salad, the leek soup, the shepherd's pie, a side of the garlicky kale, and the mixed-berry shortcake à la mode."

"Shortcake, short*cak*-in'," Mad John starting singing, taking Pearl's hand and swinging her arm. Her face blushed a deeper shade of gray.

Chevrona walked into the restaurant; I'd invited her to join us but she'd been non-committal. She nodded at everyone and sat down next to me.

"What would you like to eat?" I asked.

She indicated Zack, who was sitting on the other side of me, "I'll have what he's having."

Did I just hear the sound of a gauntlet hitting the floor?

Pearl turned to shuffle off. Mad John gave her behind a little send-off slap and a tiny high-pitched squeal of delight leapt out of her.

Abba and Josie came out from the kitchen.

"The whole family is here," Abba said. I looked at Josie, in her apron, her color high from the heat of the kitchen, and she looked so beautiful. Abba put her arm around her, "I don't know what I did before this one arrived."

"You did magic with food, is what you did," Josie said.

Zack poured everyone glasses of wine and raised his, "To Janet, who put a murderer behind bars."

"I had a lot of help."

"But, baby, you were the little engine that wouldn't quit and I am so proud of you," Zack said.

"Is Sally going to get out on bail?" I asked Chevrona.

"The judge has denied it so far, but they'll come back and ask again, of course. She's got some pretty high-powered lawyers, but all the money in the world can't undo a confession with five witnesses."

"And what about Collier Denton?"

"He may get away with murder. Sally spilled — she claims that when she went snooping at Stock's house she found Denton's credit card receipt for a gas can. But she can't produce it and the testimony of a murderer doesn't carry much weight. We are charging him and Graham Clarke with the theft of the Indian artifacts from Goat Island."

"And Pavel?"

"He gets off scot-free. There's really nothing to charge him with."

"But he gave all those pills to Natasha."

"If he had *sold* them to her, he'd be in trouble."

"What about possession?"

"He didn't actually possess them. And there was a seemingly legitimate prescription for them."

"So Pavel is going to become Mr. Octavia Bump. Move over, Horatio Alger," I said.

"You got the big fish, baby," Zack said.

"Let me get these orders up," Josie said, going back to the kitchen.

It was getting late and the place was emptying out. Abba went around and lit a few candles and put Natasha's CD on. Outside, the streets of Sawyerville were quiet. Our food arrived and everyone dug in.

I went into the kitchen. Josie was prepping the shortcakes. The back door was open and I was surprised to see Sputnik tied up on the patio, contentedly sleeping on his side.

"You've been away a lot," Josie said. "He gets lonely, I hope it's okay I brought him over."

I felt a little stab of jealousy, but nodded. Josie finished with the desserts, put them on the pass-through, and started in on kitchen clean-up. "So this is working out," I said.

She nodded, "Abba's a great boss. More like a teacher really."

I had an urge to go over and smother her in a hug and tell her how proud I was of her. Thankfully it passed.

She started to sweep the floor. "Thank you for taking a chance on me."

"I think you took the bigger chance."

Sputnik woke up and stuck his head into the kitchen; when he saw us together his tail went to wagging.

"You know, Josie . . . ?"

She stopped sweeping and looked at me, "Yeah?"

"I wanted to ask you about something . . . this is kinda hard for me . . . there are a couple of people from my past . . ."

She gave me a sympathetic, knowing smile.

"Did Abba say something to you?" I asked.

"She said a little something."

"Anyway, I'm thinking I might maybe like to try and track them down."

"I think that would be a really good thing, Janet."

"Do you think maybe —"

"I could help? You're damn right I could."

Okay, the words were officially out, the first step had been taken, I had friends along with me on the journey.

I walked out to the patio and inhaled a deep hit of the heavy Hudson Valley air.

Sputnik butted his head "hello" against me, I petted him, "Hey, buddy."

Then I went inside to help Josie scrub a few pots.

ABOUT THE AUTHOR

Sebastian Stuart's recent novel, *The Hour Between* (Alyson, 2009) won the Ferro-Grumley Award and was a National Public Radio Seasons Readings Selection. The ghostwritten *Charm! by Kendell Hart* (Hyperion, 2008) was a *New York Times* bestseller. *24-Karat Kids,* written with Dr. Judy Goldstein (St. Martins, 2006) was published in seven languages. His first novel, *The Mentor* (Bantam, 1999) was a Book of the Month Selection.

As a playwright, Sebastian was dubbed "the poet laureate of the Lower East Side" by Michael Musto in *The Village Voice.* His plays — which include *Smoking Newports and Eating French Fries, Beverly's Yard Sale,* and *Under the Kerosene Moon* — have been seen at the Public Theater, The Kitchen, and LaMama, among other venues.

Sebastian has worked as a ghostwriter and editor in every genre imaginable, from business to politics to show business to travel.

A native New Yorker, he now lives with novelist Stephen McCauley in Cambridge, Massachusetts, and Saugerties, New York.

The employees of Thorndike Press hope you have enjoyed this Large Print book. All our Thorndike, Wheeler, and Kennebec Large Print titles are designed for easy reading, and all our books are made to last. Other Thorndike Press Large Print books are available at your library, through selected bookstores, or directly from us.

For information about titles, please call:
(800) 223-1244

or visit our Web site at:
http://gale.cengage.com/thorndike

To share your comments, please write:
Publisher
Thorndike Press
10 Water St., Suite 310
Waterville, ME 04901